MICRO

#9
DEAD
RINGER

by
Chassie L. West
Programming by Susan M. Zakar

A Parachute Press Book

SCHOLASTIC INC.
New York Toronto London Auckland Sydney Tokyo

Book was designed by Gene Siegel.

ISBN 0-590-33384-4

12 11 10 9 8 7 6 5 4 3 2 1   3   5 6 7 8 9/8 0/9

Printed in the U.S.A.   01

Warning: The following information is crucial to the success of your mission. Read it carefully. It may save your life.

As a certified member of ACT (the Adventure Connection Team) your job, as always, is to defend the cause of good against evil. It won't be easy, because BRUTE (the Bureau of Random Unlawful Terror and Evil), an international organization bent on wreaking havoc throughout the world, will be fighting you every step of the way. Your computer expertise will be vital to this mission. So turn on your home system. Throughout this adventure you'll be called upon to program it to get the ACT team out of some really tough spots.

The text will tell you which micros will run each program. If the program won't run as is on your computer, consult the Reference Manual in the back of the book — fast! Good luck. This message will be erased from memory in 30 seconds.

CHAPTER
1

You push through the swinging doors of Doc Wilbur's Drug Store, anxiety nibbling around the edges of your mind. There are no customers, and Doc, who is behind the counter, nods a greeting as he peers at you over the bifocals that have slipped down his nose. Instead of your usual five-minute chat with him, you only wave, then hurry to the rear of the store to the magazine racks.

Your eyes track from one end of the display to the other. Where is it? This month's issue of *X-Men Comics* is four days late — and not just at Doc's, but everywhere else you've checked, too. No one knows the reason.

"Probably somebody on strike somewhere along the line," Doc had suggested yesterday. "Give them a day or two, they'll be here."

There was no way to explain that you can't

afford to wait that long. You've got to have that comic book! Suppose ACT has sent one of their coded messages? Without *X-Men Comics*, you would be up the creek, with no way to decode it. Sure, as ACT's computer ace, you could eventually figure out how to do it, but by the time you did, the mission would be over.

Should you contact ACT headquarters to make sure they know about the late shipment? Under normal circumstances, it would be against the rules. You call headquarters only in an emergency, and there isn't an emergency — yet. Gritting your teeth in indecision, you decide to put off that call for one more day.

You're scanning other titles — Doc carries a wide selection of computer magazines — when the tiny hairs on the back of your neck begin to stir. You thought you were alone back here, but you sense a presence nearby. Whirling around, you find yourself meeting the bright, curious gaze of a kid a few feet away. But immediately you change your description of this person. He's not a kid at all. He's a midget, one of the little people, as they prefer to be called. Dressed in a dark, three-piece suit, white shirt, and striped tie, he looks ready to go to the office. Your brain rocks with surprise. You've lived in this part of town all your life and have never seen any midgets around before.

"Hello," he says with a bright smile. "Would you mind handing me a copy of *Com-*

puter Daily?'' The small hand points toward the top shelf. "It's a little high for me."

"Sure." Trying not to stare, you take it down and offer it to him. He's half your height.

He nods a thank you. "I notice you were looking through computer magazines yourself. Do you know much about computers?" he asks, tilting his head to one side. Something about the intensity with which he looks at you puts you on your guard.

"I know a little about them," you admit warily, "but I still have a lot to learn."

"Same here," he says, nodding. "I'm having a problem with my keyboard, a few letters that aren't registering on my monitor. I'd like to fix it myself, if I can."

"Make sure your cable's connected firmly to your motherboard," you suggest. "And check for broken pins."

He nods. "I will. The problem is it doesn't happen all the time, just every now and then. The A, the C, and the T on the left side of the keyboard, for instance."

You start backing away from this small person, your heart beginning to lurch in your chest. Why did he spell out ACT? Is he an ACT agent? Or could this be a BRUTE agent? Have they caught on to you somehow?

He stops you with a surprisingly strong hand on your arm. "Look, I don't have much time, and unless we start talking about constellations, I've run out of ways to work the name Orion into the conversation. ACT sent me. If you need any further proof, last month's password was 'licorice.' ''

You relax a little, since he is right about the password. ''Who are you?''

''Just a messenger. The coordinator's really bugged with you. If you'd remembered to activate the homing signal on your micro, I wouldn't have had to hit every bookstore and magazine rack in this neighborhood trying to find you.'' He hands the computer magazine back to you. ''I won't need this. You might want to check page twenty-seven before you put it back on the rack, though.'' He turns and disappears between the shelves of bandages and first-aid supplies.

Your curiosity soaring, you open the copy of *Computer Daily*, noticing how much thicker it feels than when you first picked it up. Of course, there, tucked securely inside the magazine, is a copy of *X-Men Comics*! It's the issue you've been waiting for! He must have slipped it in there, although you could swear he didn't have anything in his hands when he first spoke to you.

You flip to the next to the last page where the decoding program is usually printed in invisible ink. A small sheet of folded paper falls to the floor. You pick it up, your fingers feeling twice as thick as usual, and unfold it. Six lines of gobbledy-gook dance across the page. It's a message from ACT!!

PTLSS GJB BEDBRQII GDHN
VCXGMSU VKI UXLARNPZG
PT QK KP WJNKCQ TIKUH FTK
UJSY
MG 0400 KPYK XHL ONXLRPPTW.
TFYZEXBO UF GBYCW

A germ of suspicion peeks from under a back corner of your mind and you hesitate, forcing yourself to stop and think. Why was the message delivered to you this way? Wouldn't it have been simpler if the man had just passed it along verbally?

Your ACT training supplies the answer to that: He obviously didn't have a need to know. This might be a "For Your Eyes Only" set of instructions.

After paying for the magazine, with the comic hidden inside, you dart around to the alley and hide behind a stack of trash cans. Digging the magazine and comic book out of the paper bag, you place the special transparency over the next to the last page. Suddenly, there it is, the short BASIC program in invisible ink that will help you decode the message.

Type the following program into your computer. Run it and enter the secret message. Line 120 must be typed as one line on your computer.

PROGRAM 1

```
100   REM  DECODER
110   GOSUB 900
120   PRINT "(TYPE 'STOP' TO END)"
      :PRINT
130   PRINT "ENTER MESSAGE:"
140   INPUT M$
150   IF M$="STOP" THEN END
160   FOR I=1 TO LEN(M$)
170   A$=M$:SB=I:SE=1:GOSUB 800
180   L$=XC$
190   IF ((L$<"A")+(L$>"Z")) THEN 250
200   KT=KT+1:IF KT>26 THEN KT=1
210   T=ASC(L$):T=T-KT
220   IF T< ASC("A") THEN T=T+26
230   PRINT CHR$(T);
240   GOTO 260
250   PRINT L$;
260   NEXT I
270   PRINT:PRINT:GOTO 130
800   XC$=MID$(A$,SB,SE):RETURN
900   HOME:RETURN
```

This program will run as is on the Apple II + and IIe. See the Reference Manual, page 117, for changes for all other computers.

The words on your monitor hit you like a punch in your middle, because this President is more than a name in the daily paper or a familiar face on television. You feel as if this President is a friend, because you've met him, spoken to him.

Sure, it was only for a few minutes last year when your honors group went to Washington and toured the White House. But suddenly there he was, the man with the big, flat feet, passing through the halls, when he saw you and came over to say hello. He shook hands with everyone, and you could swear a glimmer of recognition flared in his eyes when you told him your name. Of course, it was just your imagination running in high gear. It had to be sheer coincidence that he remarked that you looked like a class act and everyone groaned at his terrible pun. And you know now it was pure chance that he happened to be looking at you when he said it. He couldn't have known . . . could he?

You tuck the miniature computer that ACT gave you for field missions back into your pocket, this time remembering to activate the homing signal. This latest version does everything but hang up your clothes, and it's no bigger than a three-by-five index card.

Heading for the bus stop, you wonder who will make up the rest of the ACT team. Fortunately, you don't have a long wait — the C-7 bus trundles along before you've had time to conjure up an imaginary crew of experts. The bus makes good time until it gets to Third, where traffic is moving like a snail with sore feet. According to your watch, it's seven minutes to four, and you're six long blocks from your pickup point.

"What's going on?" you ask the bus driver. "It's not rush hour yet."

"Main's blocked off. Got to detour over to Central."

"But I've got to be at Third and Main in a few minutes," you blurt in desperation.

"Best you start walkin' then," he drawls, opening the door to let you out.

You take off, running full speed down Third Street, one hand on the pocket of your jacket so that your miniature computer doesn't work its way out. A peek at your watch shows that you've got four minutes and three blocks left. Will your courier wait for you? Of all days for this to happen!

The final two blocks are agony. Your breath burns in your throat and a cramp bites into your right side. Perspiration streams from your forehead, the salt stinging your eyes.

As you approach Main Street, you slow down, your eyes stretching wide with horror. The sidewalk is jammed with people standing three deep! Your ACT contact will never be able to find you in this mob!

"Here come the elephants!" someone shouts. Then you remember. The circus is leaving after a month's performance at the Civic Center.

You worm your way through to the front of the crowd where you sit down on the curb beside several little kids who squeeze over to make room for you. They peer at you curiously, as if they didn't know big kids liked the circus, too. You give them a sheepish grin, and after a second, they grin back.

The elephants are just lumbering into view from your right, each trunk looped around the tail of the one in front. Then come the tigers and lions, pacing their cages fretfully.

Next are the clowns. One, dressed like a doctor, is driving a miniature ambulance, and walking on either side are two clown nurses stuffed with pillows, so fat they look like cartoon characters. One has an enormous thermometer stuck in her pocket. The other hefts a mallet, the kind used to test your knee reflexes, only hers is the size of a sledgehammer.

As they near, the nurse with the mallet bounces in your direction, and — *whang!* — bops you on the head with her mallet. It must be made of sponge, because you barely feel it.

"Emergency!" she shrieks. "Doctor, this patient has a head wound!" The kids beside you squeal with laughter.

Immediately, the other nurse waddles over, pulls a huge roll of gauze from her dress front, and begins looping it around your head.

"Hey! Wait a minute!" you yell. The clown doctor stops the ambulance, opens the rear doors, and he and the nurse who gave you your head wound clumsily remove a stretcher. Before you can open your mouth to protest, your nurse wraps a big arm around your middle, folds you over it, and hauls you off your feet. For the first time, you suspect that your nurse is a male, considering the way you're being manhandled. There you are, your nose practically scraping the asphalt, your rear end pointing skywards. He carries you to the stretcher as if you were a rag doll. The crowd roars.

"Please," you gasp as the doctor pushes you down on the stretcher and fastens straps across your chest. "I can't go with you! I'm supposed to meet someone. They'll miss me."

"Oh, quit squawkin' and give me the password," the doctor growls, pulling a stethoscope as long as he is tall from under his white coat.

"Huh?" you croak.

He bends over, pretending to listen to your heart while his nurses flutter nearby. "Password, Orion!" he snaps.

"Oh! Uh — 'smile'!" This is your transport??

"Then do it!" he grates at you. "From here on in, you're part of the act — pardon the pun. Whoop it up, kid, or they'll take your clown license away."

Straightening, he removes the stethoscope and flings it into the rear of the ambulance. Before you can do anything, the doors slam. The siren begins to screech and the vehicle accelerates with a squeal of tires.

Smile! You are off on your mission, off to help the President.

CHAPTER
2

The ambulance races over the parade route, weaving in and out between horses and clowns on foot, past the elephants and trucks loaded with the caged animals. Before long, they are all behind you. Familiar landmarks zip past the windows. This thing is really traveling!

"Hey! Where are we going?" you yell. No one bothers to answer. There's little to do except stay put and hope that the maniac driving this rig doesn't hit something. After an eternity of speeding around corners on two wheels and hitting potholes and bumps hard enough to jar your teeth loose, the ambulance finally begins to slow down. As it stops, the rear doors are thrown open.

"Okay, we're here," your nurse says. "Sorry about all the zaniness back there. Had to make it look good. You okay?"

"I guess," you answer, sitting up and looking around to get your bearings. You're a good distance behind Union Station, somewhere in the railroad yard. Tracks snake in all directions, and to your left, a freight train is parked. "Danneman's Circus" is painted across the sides of most of the cars.

The doctor comes around as you jump out of the ambulance. "Move it, Orion. They're waiting for you. The coordinator's on a tight schedule." He takes your arm and guides you toward a car on the siding. Unlike most of the others, it's a passenger car, with curtains at the windows. Its interior isn't what you expected. The aisle runs the length of one side and a row of doors opens off it.

"The cars like this have been converted into dormitory rooms for the circus performers," the doctor explains. "It's a tight squeeze, but it's comfy."

He stops at a door marked "G" and raps out a signal: one-two-three, one-two, one-two-three-four. After a short delay, the door is thrown open and you find your nose glued to the business end of a very large revolver. It's so big that, for the moment, you have no interest in who's holding it.

The door closes, and abruptly you're jerked around to face it. "Spread 'em," a deep voice snaps. You've seen enough television to know precisely what he means and you assume the position for frisking.

13

"Come on now, Scotty," another voice says soothingly. "There's no need for that."

"The way things have been going," the frisker says as he pats your sides, "there's every need in the world. Besides, it's my job. Okay, you're clean," he says finally.

You turn around very slowly. The man in front of you, all six feet plus of him, seems poised to spring. Then he relaxes, a small smile lighting his craggy features. He's freckled from hairline to chin, with piercing blue eyes under a shock of bright-red hair. "Sorry," he offers. "It's just something I had to do." He steps aside so you can see beyond him.

There are two others in the roomette: a short, wiry man with hair the color of corn-silk, a spray of creases at the corners of his eyes, and an engaging, lopsided grin; and a very dignified gentleman in shoes so shiny they must have been polished with floor wax. When you finally get around to his face, it's someone you've met on an earlier mission.

"Senator Macklin!"

He looks as if he survived the ordeal on Corona okay, and he flashes the smile that has helped him in office for several terms. "Glad to see you again, Orion. This was a rush job, so I'm your coordinator for this mission. The gentleman who greeted you at the door is Alex Scott, a member of the Secret Service."

"Scotty," your frisker corrects him. He extends a friendly hand. "Glad to meet you."

"And this gentleman in the corner," the Senator continues, "is Wilhelm — "

"Dutch." The wiry man gets to his feet and leans to shake your hand. "I don't care what my mother named me, I don't answer to nothin' but Dutch."

You grin at him. The two of you will get along fine.

"Have a seat, Orion," Senator Macklin says. "We need to fill you in and firm up our plans. Then I'll have to bow out; I've got a train to catch." You wonder if the Senator's forgotten he's already on a train.

"The message from ACT said there was a plot against the President," you offer to get the ball rolling.

Senator Macklin's broad forehead creases in a frown. "Before this afternoon, I would have felt that 'plot' was too strong a word. But now, it could be. . . . " His voice trails off. He leans forward, elbows on his knees. "The President has just had a new computer system installed. It's called the Computerized Executive Information Network — the Net, for short."

Your heart speeds up. You'll be working on the President's own computer!

"The Net is used any number of ways," the Senator goes on. "All the President's appointments are listed on it, his travel plans, miscellaneous notes, the texts of his speeches. But that's just the beginning. It's also used to store information about defense plans, intelligence, and other supersensitive subjects, which he can call up whenever he needs to prepare himself, say, for a meeting with a head of state from another country.''

''What kind of security system does it have to keep out the hackers?'' you ask.

''Layers of passwords like you wouldn't believe,'' Scotty volunteers. ''Under normal circumstances, it takes a good five minutes to enter all the passwords to get to classified information.''

''Under normal circumstances?'' you echo.

''If there were an emergency — for instance, if the country were under attack and five minutes might make all the difference — there's a shortcut,'' Senator Macklin responds. ''But we're getting a little ahead of ourselves. Someone's been monkeying with the Net, switching the President's appointments around, fiddling with the texts of his speeches. Until recently, it was almost as if someone were playing practical jokes on him.''

''The Secret Service didn't think they were so funny,'' Scotty growls. ''Our crew drove the President to confer with a visiting ambassador, only the Net directions had us taking the President to a garbage dump, while the ambassador sat twiddling his thumbs back at the Executive Building, waiting for us.''

''And when we got to the dump,'' Scotty goes on, ''we were face-to-face with a big gizmo that picks up a load and deposits it in the compactor. There was a great big electro-magnetic disc on the end of the crane, which was hanging outside the enclosure. Somebody had left it activated and ready to snatch up anything metal. Luckily, Tanner, the driver that day, spotted it and managed to stop it in time. If he hadn't the limo would have been jerked 16 feet into the air and we could have wound up in a trash compactor! Now we don't know if this was a deliberate attempt on his life or just a prank that got a whole lot less funny.''

''And there's no way to tell who'd put those directions into the President's computer system?'' Dutch asks.

''If there were, we wouldn't have this problem,'' the Senator growls.

''How many terminals are there?'' you ask, intrigued at how complex this setup must be.

''Just three,'' Scotty supplies. ''One in the White House, one in the limo, and a port-able one that goes everywhere the President goes. But, like the Senator said, things have gotten serious. A couple of the President's speeches have been changed so he'd sound as if he'd lost his mind. Just silly stuff — a nurs-ery rhyme and one of those nonsense poems from *Alice in Wonderland*.''

''Fortunately, the President caught it be-forehand. He just spoke off the cuff,'' Senator Macklin injects. ''That put him on his guard. Then yesterday, he was reviewing the text of the announcement about the summit meeting in a couple of weeks, and discovered that someone had changed two paragraphs. Had he read them aloud during the press conference, he'd have let some top-secret defense plans out of the bag."

"Uh-oh," you reply. "Defense plans, huh? Any chance that BRUTE's got anything to do with this?"

"There's always the possibility; there's just no proof — yet." The Senator gets up and peeks out of the curtain. "The rest of the circus performers have arrived. You'll be ready to leave soon." He turns back. "It's possible that whomever we're dealing with has abandoned just trying to make the President look bad. The incident with the trash compactor could mean that now they're trying to eliminate him altogether."

"Eliminate him?" you gulp.

"As in assassinate him," Scotty supplies, taking the seat the Senator has vacated.

"The only reason I know of the existence of the Net," Senator Macklin says, "is because I'm the congressional liaison. The only people who know about this new computer system are the Vice-President, the members of the cabinet, and one or two on the President's personal staff. Are you getting my point?"

You whistle in surprise. "Yes, sir! There could be a traitor in his own backyard!"

"Right," Scotty snaps, "and there may be more than one, for all we know."

18

"The summit meeting is two weeks away," Senator Macklin says. He opens a panel in the wall and removes a coat. "If we don't clear this up before then, heaven knows what might go wrong. The President is spending this weekend on Roger Castleman's estate —"

"*Castleman*, the millionaire?" Dutch asks.

"You got it, ace," Scotty snaps.

"Castleman and the President have known each other for years," the Senator explains. "He's away more than he's home, so he lets the President use the estate whenever he's in the area."

"So that's where we're going," you muse, wondering what a millionaire's estate is like.

"The President is taking a three-day weekend and making a working vacation out of it," the Senator says. "Members of the cabinet and the Vice-President will be joining him to brief him for the summit meeting. It seems likely that the "rat," whoever he or she is, will also be there."

"But why are we on a circus train?" you ask.

"Because the President is a nut about circuses," Scotty says wearily. "When he heard that this one was scheduled to play a town nearby, he asked me to arrange for a few acts to perform on the estate for any of the visitors who'd like to see it. We — the Secret Service — don't like it. That's all we need, an estate full of clowns. We'll never know who's wearing those lightbulb noses and fright wigs.''

"But this is the only time that the Vice-President and the cabinet will be together in one place, so it's the only opportunity we'll have to ferret out the traitor in the ranks," the Senator adds.

"In three days?" you croak.

"Preferably less. You, Orion, will have to monitor the Net to watch for any interference and, if possible, try to track it to its source. Dutch is an expert on electronics and explosives. If anyone has designs on blowing the system up, he'll be the one to deal with that problem.''

"And I'm the liaison with the circus and the President's staff," Scotty says. "I'll be serving as team leader, since I know the lay of the land and all the people involved.''

"So how soon do we leave?" you ask. Before anyone can respond, someone bangs frantically at the door. Scotty snatches out his gun so fast, all you see is a blur of movement. You begin to feel sorry for the person outside.

"Shhh," Scotty orders, a finger to his lips. Grasping the knob, he yanks it open. The next second, he's hurtling backwards, shoved by a person in the doorway who is the biggest lady you've ever seen. Not only is she taller than Scotty, she's also broader, and not one bit of her looks like fat, either.

She moves in, her long purple robe

swishing in the shocked silence. Several foot-long plumes decorate her coal-black hair, and she stares around the room, eyes boring into each of you like laser rays.

"You!" she intones dramatically, a long finger aimed right at your nose, "and you" — she points at Dutch — "and you with the silly gun." The finger, with its long purple nail, stops at Scotty. "You three are in danger!" She has a heavy accent — you aren't sure what kind, but it sounds slightly Russian.

"Who are you?" the Senator demands.

Scotty, a sheepish expression on his face, is pocketing his revolver. "This is Countess Esmerelda. She's with the circus."

"One of them fortune-tellers?" Dutch asks wryly. "Knows all, sees all, tells all?" His tone makes it clear what he thinks.

"Watch it, buster!" Suddenly the accent is gone and the Countess has gone from high Russian melodrama to U.S. street talk in no time flat. Her plumes quiver with indignation and wisps fly through the air. She's shedding.

"What kind of danger?" Scotty asks.

The Senator looks shocked. "You believe her?" he asks.

The Secret Service agent clears his throat nervously. "Look, Senator, part of my job was to do a background check on everyone with the circus and — "

"What?" the lady bellows. "You've been poking around into Countess Esmerelda's pri-

vate life? How dare you!'' The accent is back, her eyes flashing. Then she grins. ''Found out I was a red-hot mama, didn't you?'' Accent — gone.

Scotty turns the color of strawberries and focuses on the Senator. ''I can't help what you think, sir. As far as psychic powers are concerned, she's no fake. Nobody could come up with a name for her gift, but she's got something.''

''You betcher booties I've got something,'' the Countess says. ''I could see the orange aura around this car from a block away. Now that I'm here, it's like looking at the three of you through a bowl of orange gelatin.'' She shudders. ''I *detest* orange gelatin.''

Dutch appears interested, despite himself. ''Orange means danger?''

She has obviously forgiven him his earlier slip. ''*Tons* of it. But your basic auras are the *loveliest* royal blues, a noble color to match your noble hearts and intentions. Under the circumstances, I simply *had* to warn you.''

Scotty squints at her. ''In other words, you can tell if a person has honorable intentions from his aura?''

''Of course,'' she says haughtily. ''The danger, by the way, is from some perfectly ghastly person named Eturbee. Does that mean anything to you?''

The Senator frowns. ''Never heard of him. You, Scotty?''

Scotty shakes his head. "No, but I'll run a check on him."

You are racking your brain, but the name means nothing. The Countess is off again and it's difficult to concentrate once she gets started. She's very dramatic, hands flying. She seems to speak in *italics!*

"I've got to go," says the Senator, interrupting her and slipping into his coat. "Countess, if Scotty vouches for your — uh, gifts, that's enough for me, so — "

"Such a *sweet* boy," she coos.

" — so I'm going to take a chance on you. These three are going on a dangerous mission. If you can sense ill will in people, you might be good to have around."

She definitely seems interested. "A mission? What kind?"

"I'm afraid I can't tell you that. Security, you know. But you can help by just keeping an eye on the team."

You have a feeling the Senator wants the team to keep an eye on the Countess, too. Pretty smart, these politicians.

"The Countess will go along to help," she agrees. "I have other abilities that have nothing to do with my gifts. Not to worry, sweetie" — she pats his cheek — "your troubles are over. The four of us will make one dynamite team."

You wish she'd used another adjective. After all, dynamite does go "boom"!

CHAPTER
3

The trip to Castleman's estate takes all night. At six the next morning, the circus people begin unloading the animals. The caravan that's going to perform for the President consists of several vans and cars, and two trucks, one hauling the big cats in their cages, the second pulling a horse trailer. Draped over the rear door is the small gray trunk of an elephant.

"That's got to be an awfully small elephant," you remark to Dutch as you join him in the station wagon with Scotty and the Countess.

"That's Babette," the Countess informs you. "She's just a baby. She doesn't know many tricks yet and this is the first time away from her mother, but the experience will be good for her."

A shrill whistle sounds. "That's it,"

Dutch says, closing and locking the door. "The signal to go. Hit it, Scotty."

Your station wagon pulls off to lead the way, with Scotty at the wheel. The Countess, smiling coyly at him, says, "It is a pleasure to have such a handsome young man as my chauffeur. I will sit closer." She moves over toward Scotty.

Luckily, the estate is only half an hour away. It's surprisingly hot for this early in the morning and fat, gray clouds roll across the sky. Halfway there, lightning begins to pop like flashbulbs and the caravan travels cautiously in and out of squall lines.

There is one detour because of a bridge under repair. Through the trees, you can just barely see that a whole span of the bridge is missing. Scotty grumbles about adding another ten minutes to the trip. "It's going to rain like crazy, and we're going to get caught in it."

The Countess wraps a meaty arm around his shoulders. "Not to worry, darling boy. You forget I know about these things. It won't rain again. Thunder, lightning, yes. Rain, no."

Scotty relaxes visibly. He certainly puts a lot of stock in what the Countess says, perhaps because she's right. The lightning increases, zigzagging across the sky more and more often and thunder joins it. But not a drop of rain.

"Countess Esmerelda," you ask timidly, "is it all right if I ask where you're from?"

The Countess looks at Scotty, then turns

in her seat to answer. "If we were alone, I would tell you Transylvania or something. But since the Secret Service has gone peeky-peeky into my background, and, since we're all on the same team and must trust one another, I will tell you the truth. I'm from Jersey City, New Jersey."

Dutch gives a shout of laughter. "Countess, you're one for the books."

"If you're from New Jersey, why do you speak with a foreign accent sometimes?" you persist.

She looks at you solemnly. "My talents are real, Orion. I did not ask for them — I was born with them. For some reason, people find it hard to accept that an ordinary person — a Myrtle Schwartz from New Jersey — could possess the kind of gifts I have. But from someone who does not talk like them, dress like them, they can accept it. So I give them what they want on the outside, which is fake, and what I have on the inside, which is not, and everybody's happy. You understand?" She gazes anxiously at you, as if your answer really matters.

"I understand." Your opinion of the Countess has gone up a notch.

The Countess peers out at the lightning. It seems to have moved closer. "The cats, they will not like this. Neither do I. I sense a threat, a danger to all of us very close by."

"We'd have been there already," Scotty

mutters, "if they hadn't been working on that bridge. It's not far, though, maybe five miles away."

It seems a long five miles, but finally he turns off the highway onto a narrow lane that winds between groves of trees and comes to a stop at a tall metal gate with a small sentry shack just inside.

"Is this it?" you ask. So far, there hasn't been much to see — just grass, trees, and more trees. Mr. Castleman's estate is well-protected, with not just one, but two high wire fences, one inside the other. The space between the two is a sort of no-man's land. The only thing in it is a guard's hut and, just outside its door, a tall, rectangular enclosure, perhaps seven feet high and four feet wide, which resembles a long packing crate set on end.

The animals stir restlessly. The weather seems to be making them nervous. Somewhere in the line, a horse whinnies anxiously.

Scotty removes what looks like a credit card from his jacket pocket. He slides it into a slit in a small metal box mounted on a sturdy pole outside the first fence. The mechanism gives a hiccup and the gate opens.

"It takes a credit card to get in?" the Countess asks.

"No, this is an identification badge. You'll each get one so you can move around the grounds without being stopped by the Secret

Service. Hi, Crenshaw,'' he says to the guard who comes out of the sentry hut.

"Scotty, that you? How'd you get off the estate without my seeing you?''

"What do you mean?'' Scotty asks. "I just got here.''

Crenshaw shakes his head in confusion. "I could swear I saw you on the grounds about an hour ago.''

"Wasn't me. What's that?'' He points to the mysterious up-ended crate.

He shrugs. "Some new kind of security thing. Everybody's got to go through it. Shouldn't take long — you just step inside, lights come on, something buzzes, and that's it. Come on in. You might as well be first.''

Scotty's about to pull through the first gate when one of the drivers runs up from the rear of the line.

"Hey, Mr. Scott, Babette's gettin' real antsy about this storm. Is it all right if we move up in line so we can take her through and into some sort of shelter?''

"Sure, drive her on up,'' Scotty says. "You can bring her through right behind us.''

The elephant's driver sprints away as thunder rumbles louder and louder.

Scotty puts the station wagon in gear and rolls through the first gate. He gets out and goes into the security stall. Fifteen seconds later, he's out, shrugging his shoulders.

"If that thing's supposed to detect metal,

it failed," he says to Crenshaw. "No alarms went off and I'm carrying my gun."

"Maybe it works differently. Doesn't matter. Everybody's got to go through. Those are my orders."

"Okay, troops," Scotty beckons. "Come on, so we can get moving."

It does seem to be a mysterious waste of 15 seconds. You step in and shut the door. Immediately, there's a hum. A ring of fluorescent lights in the ceiling lowers itself to the floor, with you in its center. Then, *swoosh*, it goes back up again. That's all there is to it.

As you get back into the car, Scotty is staring at the first gate. "Crenshaw, something wrong with that gate back there? It should have closed after we came in."

Crenshaw scowls, scratching his head in confusion. "I don't know. It was all right before."

Meanwhile, the small horse trailer in which Babette is riding has passed the others in line and approaches the outer gate, which is still wide open. Stepping out of the station wagon, Scotty waves for the truck to pass through. Almost as soon as it does, the gate begins to close.

"Maybe the lightning hit nearby and scrambled things up for a minute," Crenshaw says, moving back toward his hut. As if in response to his words, a jagged arrow of white-hot light takes aim and streaks toward the ground just over the hill on the other side of the road. It hits with an ear-shattering crack. The earth seems to move beneath your feet. Babette screams with fear and kicks the sides of the trailer with a resounding thud.

"Mr. Scott, please," her driver calls, "we need to get moving."

"Okay, you jump on in the security detector. By the time you get out, this second gate should be open." He darts to the card reader next to the inner gate, the badge in his hand.

Suddenly the Countess screams, "Scotty, no! Don't touch it!"

"Why?" He turns back to stare at her curiously.

"I — I sense a terrible danger."

"Hey, what's that noise?" you ask, having noticed the sound for the first time. You can barely hear it, unless you listen closely between peals of thunder. It's a low, ominous hum.

Scrambling from the back seat, you approach the first gate. "It's coming from here."

"Here, too," Scotty says tersely.

Dutch hops out and moves to Scotty's side. "You're right." Picking up a twig, he tosses it against the fence. Immediately, sparks spit from the fence and the twig falls, charred and smoking, to the ground. "Scotty, there's enough electricity running through these fences to light up a whole city, and stuck in here between them like this, we're sitting ducks. If these two fences get hit by lightning, even if it

30

strikes anywhere near them, these boys are going to start arcing like something in a Frankenstein movie." The sky lights up, thunder claps immediately behind it, and Babette screams again, her voice filled with fear.

"Mr. Scott," the driver of the truck shouts, "I've seen elephants go berserk in weather like this. If we don't get her to a shelter soon, she's going to destroy that trailer, and if we're anywhere near, we'll probably get stomped to death, too."

Scotty's face is grim. "Crenshaw, isn't there an override system or something?"

Crenshaw is the color of paste. "Both gates are controlled by a computer here in the shack. I don't know nothing about it — I'm just here to keep it company."

Three pairs of eyes swing toward you as Babette gives the trailer a kick hard enough to set it rocking. "Move it, Orion," Scotty snaps, "or we'll have a 500-pound elephant in our laps."

"If we don't get barbecued first," Dutch mutters.

"In here," Crenshaw says, opening the door for you. His face is wet with perspiration as he points to a metal box around three feet tall in the corner. Loosening the screws at its base, he removes the cover to reveal the computer itself. Wiggling your fingers as if in preparation for a piano concert, you attack the keyboard.

With flashes of lightning filling the interior of the small shack like explosions of a giant strobe, you scan through the listing you've requested. The shock, when you see how this program has been written, is hard to hide. Biting the inside of your cheek to remind yourself to keep a poker face, you try a simulation run.

Input the following program and run it. Lines 120, 310, 410, 420, 430, and 960 must each be typed as one line. When it asks for a name, try Scott, since Scotty is the one about to put in his ID card. Then see if you can change the program to open the gate — without frying the team. Need help? Check the Reference Manual, page 117.

PROGRAM 2

```
100   REM ELECTRIC FENCE
110   GOSUB 900:GOSUB 960:WU=5
120   READ A$:SB=1:SE=SW:GOSUB 800
      :E$=XC$
130   READ A$:GOSUB 800:N$=XC$
140   PRINT "NAME:";:INPUT M$
150   FOR I=1 TO 4:REM CHECK NAMES
160   READ X1$
170   IF X1$=M$ THEN T=11
180   NEXT I
190   HH=INT(SH/2-1):HV=INT(SH/2-1)
200   FOR I=1 TO INT(HV/2)
210   VT=HV+I:HT=1:GOSUB 910
```

```
22Ø    PRINT E$
23Ø    WT=WU:GOSUB 92Ø
24Ø    GOSUB 91Ø:PRINT N$
25Ø    WT=WU:GOSUB 92Ø
26Ø    NEXT I
27Ø    IF T=1 THEN 3ØØ:REM OPEN GATE
28Ø    GOTO 2ØØ
29Ø    BL$=""
3ØØ    FOR I=1 TO 6
31Ø    A$=BL$:B$=" ":GOSUB 82Ø
       :BL$=A$
32Ø    B$="!":GOSUB 82Ø
33Ø    FOR J=1 TO INT(HV/2)
34Ø    VT=HV+J:HT=HH:GOSUB 91Ø
35Ø    PRINT A$;
36Ø    NEXT J
37Ø    WT=WU*1Ø:GOSUB 92Ø
38Ø    NEXT I
39Ø    VT=SH-2:HT=1:GOSUB 91Ø
4ØØ    END
41Ø    DATA
       --------------------------------
       ------------
42Ø    DATA
       /////////////////////////////
       ////////////
43Ø    DATA SCOTT,MACKLIN,JONES,
       WALTON
8ØØ    XC$=MID$(A$,SB,SE):RETURN
82Ø    A$=A$+B$:RETURN
9ØØ    HOME:RETURN
91Ø    VTAB(VT):HTAB(HT):RETURN
92Ø    FOR WS=1 TO WT:NEXT WS
96Ø    NU$=CHR$(Ø):SW=4Ø:SH=24:
       KZ=-16384:KW=-16368:RETURN
```

This program will run as is on the Apple II+ and IIe. See the Reference Manual, page 118, for changes for all other computers.

Minutes later, you've done all you can do. You run the program, listening with relief as you hear the metallic grunt of the mechanism that opens the gates. As you step out of the hut, the inner fence moves aside.

Dutch hops into the station wagon and drives it through, out of the way of the truck behind it.

"Why don't you ride with him and show him the way, Dutch?" Scotty calls. "I want to stay and check out these card readers."

"I will go with them, too," the Countess says, hopping out with surprising grace, considering her size.

"Why don't you catch a ride in one of the others, Orion?" he asks.

You shake your head. "No, I'll wait for you."

He eyes you curiously, but says nothing. After making sure that the card reader is operating correctly, he sees the remainder of the caravan through the two gates. "I guess we can leave. Sure, now the sun's coming out." The two of you climb into the station wagon. "Hope you have an easier shift from here on," he calls to Crenshaw as he drives away, making certain the gate closes behind him. "Okay, what is it, Orion?"

Up to this point, you've been practically bursting to tell him, yet now that the time has come, you wish you didn't have to. "The instructions in the programming back there were for both fences to become electrified the instant you — and a list of some others — inserted your ID card into the reader."

Scotty stops the station wagon and turns to stare at you. "You're kidding! But that means that — "

"You'd have been dead before you hit the ground. I figure the only reason it didn't work was because of the lightning."

He looks up at the sky, his lips pressed tight into a thin, hard line. The storm clouds are moving off to the east. "Who else was on the list?"

"I don't remember all of them, a Jones, uh — Walton, and Senator Macklin."

"But he's not even supposed to be coming," Scotty protests.

"Maybe not, but somebody's taking no chances. That's not all, though. The program was set up so that whenever one of those cards was used, that particular set of instructions would be wiped out until the next card was inserted. Then it would immediately be activated again."

Scotty shakes his head. "I don't understand."

"Well, after a person had been killed, someone would certainly check the computer to see if that's where the problem was, don't you think? But there wouldn't be anything to see, because that part of the programming would have disappeared for the time being. We're dealing with a pro here.''

"A pro who seems to want a lot of us dead,'' Scotty says, his expression grave.

You nod as a chill of fear runs down your spine. Scotty has confirmed what you were beginning to suspect — that your life is in danger, too.

CHAPTER
4

After Scotty has made certain that the circus performers have found their quarters, he issues you an identification badge and the four of you start off on a stroll around the grounds. Castleman's estate has everything you could want — a pool, tennis courts, a stable and horses, a shooting range, a lake with boats and fishing gear, a helipad, and a golf course. The guest cabins, one for you and one for Dutch, are decorated luxuriously and outfitted with a TV, VCR, stereo — the works!

"If this is how millionaires live," Dutch grumbles, "I'm going to change my line of business."

Some of the President's guests have already arrived and are by the pool or horseback riding. Scotty waves to a couple of members of the cabinet, and even introduces a few of his fellow agents and presidential staff aides. You watch the Countess to see how her aura detector is working. She says very little, however, which worries you. The Countess usually talks nonstop.

As Scotty leads you toward the Castleman house, the Countess bows out, her face very pale. "I don't feel well," she says in apology. "I think I'll go back to our quarters and take a nap."

"You want me to swipe a golf cart and drive you back?" Dutch asks, eyeing her with concern.

"No, no. It's not that bad. I'll walk. It is good for me."

"Well, if you need us, just give us a call on your communicator," Scotty reminds her, "and we'll be there on the double."

Scotty stares after her as she leaves. "Hope she'll be all right. I'll check when we're finished." He points directly ahead. "There's Castleman's home."

The "home" stops you in your tracks, your mouth open. "Holy cow!" Dutch says in awe, because Mr. Castleman has built himself — what else? — a castle, with turrets and towers, a drawbridge and moat. Looking at it makes you feel as if you've stumbled into a time warp, that knights in armor will probably come galloping up at any minute.

"Does it have a dungeon and a dragon, too?" you croak.

Scotty grins. "Probably does. Castleman likes things to be authentic. Come on." You cross the bridge and go around to the rear of the castle. There, at the bottom of the knoll, sits a building as contemporary in design as the castle is not. All glass, brick, and soaring angles, it nestles on the lush lawn as if it has taken root there.

"This is the computer complex," Scotty explains as he inserts his ID badge into a card reader beside the door. One large glass pane slides open. "You two better insert your badges, too," he advises, "so that your presence is recorded. Now you'll be able to come in any time. Guard those badges with your life. I mean that literally," he adds solemnly.

The lobby is impressive, with cool marble floors and massive plants hanging from a ceiling two stories high. Scotty crosses to a pair of elevators. "The computers are below ground and the elevator on the right is the only one that will take you down there. The other one goes to the upper floors."

Beside the elevator is another card reader and Scotty nods to indicate you should use your badge. The door slides open onto plush carpets and paneling, seats that fold against the side walls, and classical music coming from hidden speakers.

The agent points to a keypad where the floor buttons would normally be. "You have to punch in a special code to get to the basement, or the car won't move. The code is — '' Instead of saying it aloud, he demonstrates by holding up his fingers to indicate 3, 2, 7, and 5. ''That's just in case this car is bugged,'' he says softly. ''A new code is used any time the President is here. Not even Castleman's staff knows what it is. Memorize it.''

You nod and push 3–2–7–5. The elevator doors close and then you sense its movement, but it is so smooth that it's difficult to tell that you're going down at all. ''Sure is slow,'' you observe when after 15 seconds it's still going down.

Scotty chuckles. ''That's what you think. If I told you how far below ground you are, you wouldn't believe me.''

The door eases open onto soft, blue-green walls that glow as if bathed in sunshine. Like the speakers in the elevator, the source of the light is hidden. Scotty leads you to the right, past several closed doors.

''Better count the doors so you'll know your way when you come alone.'' At the sixth door, he points to yet another card reader. ''Might as well clock yourself in, so it'll admit you the next time. You, too, Dutch.''

The three of you use your badges, and each time the door opens silently and closes very quickly, giving you barely enough time to slip in.

Your eyes widen when you see the contents of the room. It houses massive computers that couldn't be any more up-to-date if they'd come off the assembly line this morning. Dutch gives a whistle of amazement. "Wow!" you breathe. "Double wow!"

"Don't get your hopes up," Scotty warns. "These boys are the heart of Castleman's empire. They keep track of each dotted 'i' and crossed 't' in every business he owns, and he owns hundreds of them. The President's terminal is back here."

He moves to the rear of the room where one wall has been painted in a brown-and-beige checkerboard pattern. "Watch carefully. Stand dead center of this wall. Count down four brown squares from the ceiling and place your badge against it."

You follow his instructions and *swishhh,* a portion of the wall slides open to reveal a hidden room. One lone terminal sits dead center on a long wooden table, along with a monitor, a printer, and a telephone.

"Don't let it fool you just because it isn't as big and flashy as the ones in the other room," Scotty says. "The Net's nothing to sneeze at."

Dutch only stifles a yawn. "Since computers aren't my bag, I think I'll head back to the entertainment compound. I want to check on the Countess. Guess I'm kind of worried about her."

Scotty nods. "I am, too. I'll be there shortly. I just want to introduce Orion to the Net."

"Well, say hello for me, too," Dutch says with a wave and starts to leave. "Oh, what's the code in the elevator to get back to the lobby?"

"Same one we used to come down."

"Terrific. See ya later." Dutch places his badge against the proper square of brown paint and the wall opens.

"Okay, Orion, just log on using your code name. We might as well check to see what kind of entries have been made in the last 24 hours."

"All right." Pulling up the one chair in the room, you type O–R–I–O–N.

It responds immediately. "Welcome, Orion. What can I do for you?"

You request a directory of entries made since noon yesterday. Each has a short title and the time it was entered recorded beside it. "Meeting, L. Briggs," you read. "Update, Sec. Walton. Directions to estate." That last one stops you. "Scotty, the President's been here before, hasn't he?"

"Sure, lots of times. Why?"

"Uh — nothing, I guess." You load the Directions file and read it. It is precisely what the title says, except that. . . . "Where's the President coming from, to get here, I mean?"

"Tylerton. That's just beyond where we

got off the train. He had a speaking engagement there. Something up?"

Biting your lip, you respond, "I'm not sure. He's coming in a car?"

Scotty stops what he is doing and concentrates on your questions. "Yes, in the limo."

"So his driver would be taking the same roads to get here as we did, right?"

The agent is losing patience. "Yes. Stop stalling, Orion. What's wrong?"

"I think somebody's after the President again. Someone is playing a nasty trick with the directions from Tylerton. Let me show you."

Input the following program and run it. Lines 130, 190, 220, 290, 410, and 960 must each be typed as one line.

PROGRAM 3

```
100   REM  ROUTE CHECK
110   READ R1$,R2$,R3$:ZZ=0
120   GOSUB 900:GOSUB 960:GOSUB 970
130   VT=1:HT=1:GOSUB 910:PRINT
      "SHOWING ROUTE"
140   VT=2:GOSUB 910:PRINT "AIRPORT";
150   HT=8:VT=2:GOSUB 910
160   A$=R1$:GOSUB 240
170   A$=R2$:GOSUB 240
180   IF ZZ<>1 THEN 210
```

```
190    VT=1:HT=1:GOSUB 910:PRINT
       "ROUTE CHECKED";
200    END
210    PRINT "ESTATE"
220    VT=1:HT=1:GOSUB 910
       :PRINT "TESTING ROUTE"
230    ZZ=1:GOTO 150
240    FOR F=1 TO LEN(A$)
250    SB=F:SE=1:GOSUB 800
260    IF XC$<>"C" THEN 330
270    F=F+1:SB=F:GOSUB 800:NS$=XC$
280    IF ((NS$<>"#")+(ZZ<>1)) THEN 310
290    PRINT "SPLASH!!":VT=1:HT=1
       :GOSUB 910
300    PRINT "DISASTER ON ROUTE!":END
310    IF ZZ=1 THEN NS$="."
320    GOTO 380
330    IF XC$="N" THEN VT=VT-1
340    IF XC$="S" THEN VT=VT+1
350    IF XC$="E" THEN HT=HT+1
360    IF XC$="W" THEN HT=HT-1
370    GOSUB 910:PRINT NS$;
380    WT=WU:GOSUB 920
390    NEXT F
400    RETURN
410    DATA
       C!SSC-EEEEC!SSSSC-WWWC!SSSC
       -EEEE
420    DATA EEEEC!SCBSC#SCBSC-EEE
430    DATA C!SCBSSSC-EEE
800    XC$=MID$(A$,SB,SE):RETURN
820    A$=A$+B$:RETURN
900    HOME:RETURN
910    VTAB(VT):HTAB(HT):RETURN
```

44

```
920    FOR WS=1 TO WT:NEXT WS
960    NU$=CHR$(Ø):SW=4Ø:SH=24:
       KZ=-16384:KW=-16368:RETURN
970    WU=1ØØ:RETURN
```

*The program will run as is on the Apple
II+ and IIe. See the Reference Manual, page
120, for changes for all other computers.*

"These directions will take the President
across the bridge."

"The bridge is out," Scotty replies.
"Don't worry about it. There's no way Larson
can miss the detour signs."

"That's just it. The directions specifi-
cally say that Larson should ignore the detour
signs because the bridge work has been com-
pleted, but the road workers haven't removed
the signs yet."

Scotty's eyes narrow as he squints at the
screen. "That's stupid! Do they think Larson's blind?"

"Look at it this way," you suggest.
"Larson is given a printout. He reads it and it
says ignore the signs. When he gets to the
signs, he'll sail right on past them. Wasn't there
a hard right just after the signs and then the
bridge?"

"That's right," Scotty confirms.

"Since you were driving, you couldn't
take the time to look, but it's the very begin-

ning of the bridge that's out, a great big gap of maybe 25 feet. If Larson trusts these directions, ignores the signs, and makes that sharp right, it'll already be too late. He'll be taking a nosedive into the river, and that was a long drop! They'll never survive it!''

"The limo should have left Tylerton five minutes ago,'' he snaps as he checks his watch. "I'll try to get Larson on my walkie-talkie.''

He tugs at the mechanism hanging on a clip from his belt, yelps, and snatches his hand away. There is a deep gash across his right index finger and it's bleeding freely. ''Ouch! There's a sharp edge on this clip. I keep meaning to get a new one.'' He digs a handkerchief from his pocket and wraps it around the finger. Carefully this time, he removes the walkie-talkie from the clip and extends the aerial.

"ER-4 calling AL-1, ER-4 calling AL-1.'' All he gets in response is static. ''This building is insulated. I've got to get outside. You stay here and see if anything else has been tampered with in the Net.''

"Sure,'' you answer, your focus on the task at hand.

Taking no chances, you check all the other entries made in the last 24 hours. They seem innocent enough. Finally you log off, and leave to go look for Scotty, hoping he was able to reach Larson on his walkie-talkie.

You keep wondering who is so determined to kill the President and why. There's still no indication that BRUTE is involved, but you're sure they're in the picture somewhere.

In the elevator, you key in 3–2–7–5. Your finger, however, does not hit the last digit squarely, sort of sliding off so that you might have hit the 6 instead. Taking no chances, you push the cancel button and punch 3–2–7–5 again. Slowly, smoothly, the car begins to move. You begin to whistle. There's something about this padded cell that makes you edgy — perhaps because it's so difficult to tell whether you're going up or down.

Finally it stops. The doors slide open and you're staring at blue-green walls again. This is not the lobby, but where is it? Scotty said this elevator ran from the main floor to the basement. And you could have sworn it had moved.

You key in 3–2–7–5. Nothing happens. The doors don't even close. You try again. Still nothing. Will you be stuck in this basement the rest of your life?

Perhaps the best thing to do is wait for Scotty back in the room with the terminal. You leave the elevator, count the doors, and insert your badge into the card reader. You start past the bank of computers and suddenly stop. Something's wrong here. There aren't as many of them as there were before, and looking more closely, you see that they aren't even the same kind. These are older. You're in the wrong room.

You go back to the elevator and start again, but find yourself returning to the same room. "What the heck's going on here?" you mutter. Maybe it's not just the wrong room, but the wrong floor as well. Except that there isn't supposed to be anything below the basement.

You walk back to the checkerboard wall, where a clipboard is hanging on a nail. On it is a list of initials — AS-1, BW-4, MR-6, a full page of them. Some have check marks next to them. You can't make any sense of them.

You place your badge on the proper square and the entrance appears. The room beyond is the same size as before, except that instead of the President's terminal, this one has four long, padded tables like the ones in doctors' offices, a row of lockers that line the wall to your right, and a door in the rear.

Two of the tables are occupied. On one, a man is lying on his back, covered with a sheet from chin to ankles. All you can see clearly are the soles of his shoes. The pattern that crisscrosses the bottoms looks like those of running shoes. At his head are several machines, perhaps monitors, because one has a small square screen, and a blip scans from one side to the other.

The man on the second table is uncovered, but he's on his side with his back to you. He, too, is connected to a monitor, and a third man is bending over him, a stethoscope around his neck. This must be an infirmary of some kind. You wonder why Scotty didn't mention the fact that there was a subbasement, and why you suddenly have the feeling that you shouldn't be here.

Slowly, you step back into the computer room, and to your surprise, the door begins to close by itself. Just before it's completely shut, you hear a voice yell, "Hey!" There's nothing particularly threatening about the word, but for some reason, you decide you had better make tracks.

You get out of that room as fast as you can, sprint toward the elevator, dart in, and punch 3–2–7–5. Nothing happens. You punch it in again. The doors begin to close just as you hear the sound of running footsteps. In the last moment before the two panels meet, a man reaches the elevator. He extends a broad flat hand as if to prevent the door from closing, but it's too late. You almost consider trying to open it for him, except that in the other hand he's holding a very large gun. Then you're sealed in and the car is moving, and your legs are feeling a bit shaky. Perhaps you should have let him in and explained how you happened to be there, except you aren't sure how you did wind up there.

Up in the lobby, you step out cautiously.

The big marble space is empty. At the door, you use your badge to get out. You stand for a second to get your bearings and wonder where Scotty is. Perhaps he went to check on the circus. "Past the castle," you mutter, trying to remember the route back to the entertainment complex, "and the tennis courts, then bear right."

You take off at a trot, running toward the castle. Just as you reach the top of the knoll on which it sits, you look back at the computer building to see a figure in a dark suit burst out of the door and look around. You step behind a tree, because it looks like the man who tried to get on the elevator. His head whips from side to side, as if he were looking for someone — you! And in his right hand, he still holds that gun!

CHAPTER
5

You make a fast dash through the trees toward the site where the circus is setting up. The entertainment complex is a small outdoor amphitheater covered by a high wooden roof. Banks of seats rise on three sides of the stage on which one large ring has been centered. The level of activity around it reminds you of an ant farm. Toward the rear of the stage, the supports for the wire-walk act are going up, and on the catwalk above, technicians are focusing the lights.

Dutch is at the side of the stage, tools in hand, adjusting a small motor that lies on its side. Working your way down to the stage, you tap him on the shoulder.

"Dutch, have you seen Scotty?"

He straightens up. "He's here somewhere, looking for you. Where've you been?"

"In the computer building. Why?"

"Scotty said he couldn't find you, thought you might have come back here. You'd better go check in with him. Last time I saw him he was headed in that direction." He points to the opposite side of the stage.

"Okay. Thanks, Dutch." You search there and in the wings. No Scotty. He's not backstage, either. You finally find him outside, behind the theater, talking to a man in a three-piece suit. Since the man is wearing a walkie-talkie, you figure he's another agent. Your team coordinator is wearing a very large bandage on his index finger.

He turns, sees you, and his worried face clears. "Well for Pete's sake, where have you been? I came back to tell you I'd reached Larson, and you were gone. I was just about to round up a few of the boys to go looking for you."

"I left around 15 minutes after you did," you explain, "but I got all confused by that elevator. You didn't tell me there was a subbasement, and that's where I wound up."

"What?" He looks at you as if you have two heads.

You lower your voice and choose your words carefully, since the second agent is listening hard, even though he's trying to look as if he isn't. There's no way to tell how many of the other Secret Service men know about your operation. "It's a long story. Anyway, I thought I ought to tell you that I stumbled into the infirmary, and I guess I shouldn't have been down there, because a guy came after me with a gun.''

Scotty shakes his head as if to loosen the cobwebs. ''Wait a minute. You aren't making any sense.''

The other agent taps Scotty on the shoulder. ''Well, since you won't be forming a search party, I'd better get moving.''

''Oh, sure. Thanks, Jarvis,'' Scotty says. ''See you later.'' He turns back to you as Jarvis strides away. ''Orion,'' he says softly, ''I didn't know about a subbasement or an infirmary. The blueprints the Secret Service were supplied don't show anything below the basement. Are you sure you weren't just turned around down there?''

''Positive.'' You describe what happened on the elevator, the computers you saw, and the people in the infirmary. ''Oh! I just realized who the man on the table was. It was the Vice-President!''

''Couldn't have been,'' Scotty says firmly. ''He's not due until later this evening.''

''Maybe not, but I could swear it was him — bald head, and he was wearing running shoes. The papers are always talking about how Vice-President Loggins wears them practically all the time.''

''Something's not right here. What did the man with the gun look like?''

''Your height, curly black hair, navy suit.

That's about all I saw — oh, except a lot of hair on the backs of his hands."

Scotty seems puzzled. "Sounds a lot like Grantly. He's Secret Service, too. He's not scheduled to work this weekend. I'd better go see if something special is up." He starts away. "Stay here for the time being," he says over his shoulder. "If you have to leave, tell Dutch where you're going."

"Okay. Hey, how's the Countess?" you call.

Scotty holds up the wounded finger and makes a face at all the gauze wrapped around it. "Just fine. She bandaged my cut for me. She's over there by the clowns." He jogs around the side of the theater and disappears from view.

There is as much activity here behind the stage block as there is out front: performers rehearsing, the trainer taking the cats through their paces, the clowns testing their routines. Turning in the direction the agent had pointed, you see the Countess across the way in a bright-red gown with gold stars all over it. She seems to be okay, and you start over to speak to her. Suddenly she turns, spots you, and even from 50 yards away, you can see the blood drain from her face. She holds up her hands and shakes her head vehemently, signaling you not to come.

Suddenly, you're aware of the *thrum* of an engine off to your left, a sound that seems to be getting louder and louder. Glancing that way, you see the ambulance that had transported you to the train station rolling toward you. And there's no one at the wheel! One of the clowns is chasing it, and it's obvious from the expression on his face that this is no joke. He is in a panic! "Watch out!" he's yelling. "Watch out!"

You're nobody's fool, you know there's no way you can jump into the driver's seat as it goes by, so you backpedal to get out of its path. It doesn't work. The darned thing swerves just enough so that it's still coming straight at you. You back up again, and move off at an angle. It veers right again and now you're sure. That ambulance is after you!

You take off — running for your life. It follows right behind you, with half the members of the circus chasing it, shouting and screaming. It would make a great act, except you suspect that if it catches you, the ending won't be funny at all. A quick look around proves there's nothing close you can use as a barrier, unless. . . .

On the far left side is a big stack of hay bales. You head for it, your heart pounding. There's no time to check behind you to see how close the vehicle is and no real need; the sound of its little engine purrs louder and louder in your ears.

"Jump!" you hear the Countess yell.

That's just what you have in mind, but you don't have breath enough to tell her so. You also suspect that time has run out. The bales of hay are a good five feet away but the ambulance is only three feet behind you and closing. The hay is piled about four feet high. You've never tried the high jump or long jump before, but if you're going to survive this, you'll have to do a combination of both.

You dig in a heel, go into a deep crouch, and launch yourself forward as if you were being catapulted toward the sky. It works. You clear the bales and land with a thud, eyes closed tight. You lie there for a long moment, waiting to feel the broken bones. But you must not have any — at least no particular part of you is shrieking with pain — so you open your eyes and find yourself looking up at the underside of a large gray chest, a jaw, and the trunk of a baby elephant. Babette lowers her head, peers at you curiously, and probes you gently with the tip of her long snout. You scurry out from under her in record time.

"Orion, you all right?" Dutch is peering over a bale.

"I'm fine — I think." The ambulance has plowed into the other side of the bales and sits, its engine grumbling and sputtering, with clowns swarming all over it. "What's wrong with that thing?" you demand. "It could have killed me!"

"I'll check." Dutch turns away and pries up the hood of the little vehicle, just as the Countess arrives on your side of the barrier. Before you can move, you're being smothered in red silk, or satin, or whatever it is.

"Oh, my poor little genius, you are safe! I'm so sorry I didn't sense the danger sooner!" She strokes your forehead, pats your back, then kisses your cheek with such fervor that the sound of it leaves your ears ringing. "Dutch, how could the ambulance go off on its own like that? It's never done it before!"

Dutch pulls his head from under the hood and points to something in its innards. "A remote-control device. It had to be something like that." He looks at you thoughtfully. "You know what this means, don't you?"

There's no need to answer him. Someone wanted you mashed into the dust. Who? And why? You gaze around, trying to gauge the reactions of the onlookers. There is only concern on the faces of the circus people and your teammates. But standing at the side of the stage block, his expression unreadable, is the agent to whom Scotty was talking. Turning swiftly, he walks away. You make a mental note to ask Scotty about him.

The Countess has one large arm still wrapped around your neck, and Babette is investigating the contents of your pockets. Wriggling out of the grasp of both, you excuse yourself. "I'm going to my cabin and wash up."

Dutch hands you a communicator. "Keep this on you and yell if anything else happens." He looks around. "I'll call Scotty and tell him about this. You watch your step.''

''You bet.'' Peering over your shoulder every two feet, you walk quickly back to your cabin. It's an A-frame with a spacious living room, kitchen, and eating area in the front. Two bedrooms and one big bath, which can be entered from either bedroom, take up the rear. In the closet of one bedroom you find two complete changes of clothes, exactly your size, too.

Locking the door between the bathroom and the second bedroom, you peel out of your dirty top and jeans and take a long, hot shower. By the time you're finished, not only are you squeaky clean, but some of the aches and pains from your record-setting leap seem to have eased. And once in the clothes provided for you, you feel like a new person.

You're about to put your wet towel and dirty clothes in the hamper in the bathroom when you hear a noise from the other bedroom, a small noise, one that raises the hair on the nape of your neck. You freeze. If it had been any of your teammates, they'd have called out to let you know they were there. Besides, you locked the front door.

The first thing you do is turn on the shower again, then carefully, quietly, you leave the bathroom. Your own bedroom is empty, as is the living room. Grateful for the wall-to-wall carpeting in the living-dining area, you sidle over to the door of the second bedroom, which is ajar. Peering in, you see Scotty standing with his back against the wall next to the bathroom door.

You frown, wondering what he's doing. Who does he think is in there? Why didn't he let you know he'd come in?

He reaches under his jacket and removes his gun. With his hand holding the weapon at shoulder height, he reaches for the knob. Suddenly, you shudder. You can see both his hands very clearly. There's no bandage on the index finger of his right hand! And there's no sign of the deep gash you saw not an hour ago. This person certainly looks like Scotty — but he isn't Scotty. And whoever he is, you know he means *you* no good.

You lean in to pull the bedroom door closed, intending to lock him in, but he sees you. Since he's got a gun, you figure this is no time for heroics. Running back into your bedroom, you slam the door behind you, lock it, and prop a chair under the knob for insurance. Your plan, such as it is, is to climb out a window.

You grab your jacket from the bed, and the bedroom door seems to shatter from the impact of a kick. "Holy cats!" you yelp. You've seen doors kicked in before, but this one shatters. It now looks like a bunch of toothpicks! With that kind of strength to deal with, you figure he's probably going to get you sooner or later. The most you can do is try to make it as much later as possible.

Adrenaline coursing through your body, you dash into the bathroom, close and lock that door, even though it's a meaningless gesture. The room is hot and steamy, the shower still on at full blast.

The window opens easily enough, but because it's higher than other windows in the cabin, getting out of it will take a few more precious seconds than you can afford. You step up onto the clothes hamper, sit on the windowsill, and manage to get one leg out when — *crack!* — the bathroom door flies open, the lock shattered. The Scotty look-alike stands in the opening. He seems 10 feet tall. As frightening as his strength is, what's more unnerving is that from the very first moment you spotted him in the bedroom until now, his face has been absolutely without expression. He might as well be a zombie!

He shoves his gun back into the holster, which makes you feel a little better, until he crosses the space in three long strides and reaches for you. Drawing your leg back, you kick out at him and catch him squarely in the abdomen. Suddenly, his arms still stretched toward you, he begins to hurtle backwards. He crashes through the doors of the shower stall and ends up sitting inside, his back against the wall. Oddly enough, he does not move.

You know you should escape while there's a chance, but curiosity wins out over common sense. Climbing down from the window, you cross to the shower stall. Scotty's double is still immobile, the hot water streaming down on him.

You reach up and turn the water off. Stooping down, you peer at him. He doesn't seem to be unconscious, but he hasn't moved a finger. In fact, you can't even see him breathing.

"CPR," you mutter under your breath. "Got to try CPR." But first things first. Gingerly, you reach in and remove his gun and toss it through the door back into the bedroom. Next, you dig out your communicator and flip it on. "Dutch, Scotty, help! I'm in my cabin."

"Be right there," Dutch responds immediately.

"I come, too!" the Countess bellows. Somehow, you're not surprised that there's no response from Scotty.

You turn your attention to his double, becoming aware for the first time of the smell of something electrical burning, and tiny crackling sounds. They seem to be coming from under his shirt somewhere. You open his jacket and start to unbutton his shirt. His chest is hairless. You unbutton as far as you can, then try to yank his shirt from his trousers, but the tail of it seems to be caught on something. Snatching his belt open, you undo the button of his slacks and then sit back on your heels, your chin dropping with surprise. There, in his navel, is a button, a bright-red button.

Getting to your feet, you back off a few steps, your mind whirling with the memory of an earlier mission. You've seen things like him before! "Oh, not again," you groan, wishing you were somewhere else. What were these things called?

Bending over the figure again, you push his belly button. Immediately, the man begins to move, so you push it again quickly to turn him off. He slumps back, immobile.

You hear tires squeal, doors slam, and Dutch and the Countess call from the living room. "Orion, where are you?"

"In the bathroom," you call.

"What happened? Will you look at this door?" Dutch says with astonishment. Then his head appears in the bathroom doorway. "What? Are you all right? Who's that?"

The Countess comes in behind him. "Scotty?" she screeches. "What have you done to him?"

"Turned him off," you reply bitterly. "This isn't really Scotty. I'm afraid something must have happened to him — the real Scotty, I mean — because this one isn't human." You look back at your teammates. "This thing's an android. A diordna, they call it."

"They? Who's *they*?" Dutch asks.

"Who else?" you say through clenched teeth. "BRUTE."

CHAPTER
6

"No wonder Scotty didn't answer when I tried to call him on the communicator. They must have captured him," Dutch says dryly.

"Now wait just a minute," the Countess says in a flat New Jersey twang. "I'm the first to admit I'm no spring chicken. I was a nurse in the Korean War, was married four times, widowed three, and done this and that, but in all that time, I've never heard of a diordna — and I thought androids were pure science fiction."

"I wish they were," you respond. "That's why the guard at the gate thought he'd seen Scotty on the estate before we arrived. And now I know what that infirmary in the subbasement really was."

"What infirmary?" Dutch asks. "What are you talking about, Orion?"

You run through your adventures in the computer building for them, winding up with the clipboard full of initials. "What scares me is the number of check marks that were on that clipboard. I didn't count them, but there's got to be more than a dozen of these androids wandering around this place."

"Well, thank heaven for that!" the Countess says fervently. She leans against the wall as if her legs might give out.

"What? Countess, you feel all right?" Dutch asks.

"I didn't before, but I certainly do now. You're right, Orion, there are a lot of these things walking around. This morning when Scotty took us on the tour, I got no vibrations, no auras at all from over half the men we saw." Her eyes roll to the ceiling. "I was terrified! I thought I'd lost my gift."

"Ahhh," Dutch replies, beginning to see the light. "That's why you looked so sick. Well, now you know your gift is workin⁊. What do we do now, Orion? You're the only one who knows anything about these fakers."

"Well, if this one is like the one we met on the space mission, he's computerized. We need to find out what his orders are and who's controlling him."

The Countess wrinkles her nose. "Is something burning?"

"It's him." You point to the android. "All that water may have short-circuited him."

"Let's find out," Dutch suggests eagerly, rubbing his hands together in anticipation.

It takes all three of you to get the thing out of the shower stall and to prop him up against the side of the tub. Dutch strips off the android's jacket and shirt. It requires a really close look before you detect the almost invisible line that forms a square in the middle of his torso.

"There it is!" you shout triumphantly. "I need something to pry him open. Countess, do you have a nail file?"

"Coming right up." She digs in a purse that's big enough to contain a roomful of furniture and whips out the file. Even with its help, it takes a full five minutes of probing and prying before you finally hear a *snap* of something breaking and the flap in his chest drops open. The burning smell becomes stronger.

Dutch gives a long whistle. "Boy, this thing is a marvel! Will you look at those circuits! But I sure don't see no computer."

You peek closely at the thing's interior and finally spot a place for a jack. "There's the link I need." Removing your portable ACT computer and unwinding the cord from the back of it, you insert the jack into the android's chest and flip the ON switch. Nothing happens.

"Yeah, he short-circuited, all right," Dutch affirms. "We got to dry him out. Countess, check under the sink. If this john is outfitted like mine next door, there should be a hair dryer under there.''

The Countess reaches in and pulls it out. "Good grief, you could open an appliance store with all this stuff.''

Dutch takes the dryer and goes to work. Before long, the burning smell has disappeared and the wires and chips appear to be dry. "Okay, try it again.''

You flip a switch and your display lights up. "Now to see how he's programmed. . . .'' You are surprised at how easy it is to get a listing of the master program.

Input the following program and run it. Lines 230, 250, 940, 950, and 960 must each be typed as one line.

PROGRAM 4

```
100   REM   TERMINAL LOGIN
110   GOSUB 960:GOSUB 970:GOSUB 900
120   READ M:K2=1
130   PRINT "ENTER THE PASSWORD"
140   READ B$
150   GOSUB 940:T=T+1
160   IF T>WU THEN 230
170   IF KY$=B$ THEN 200
180   IF KY$<>NU$ THEN 230
190   GOTO 150
200   K2=K2+1:IF K2>M THEN 250
210   READ B$
220   GOTO 150
```

```
230   GOSUB 900:PRINT "SO LONG
      BUDDY!"
240   END
250   VT=INT(SH/2):HT=INT(SW/2)-4
      :GOSUB 910
260   S=INT(WU/1.5)
270   FOR WT=WU*10 TO 1 STEP -S
280   GOSUB 900:GOSUB 910
290   PRINT "  BRUTE "
300   GOSUB 920:GOSUB 910
310   PRINT "LIVES!!!"
320   GOSUB 920
330   NEXT WT
340   GOSUB 900:GOSUB 910
350   HT=4:VT=VT-1:GOSUB 910
360   PRINT " LOGON  "
370   VT=VT+1:GOSUB 910
380   PRINT "COMPLETE."
390   END
400   DATA 6,O,R,A,N,G,E
900   HOME:RETURN
910   VTAB(VT):HTAB(HT):RETURN
920   FOR WS=1 TO WT:NEXT WS
940   KY$=NU$:KY=PEEK(KZ) :IF
      KY<128 THEN RETURN
950   KY$=CHR$(KY-128):POKE KW,0
      :RETURN
960   NU$=CHR$(0):SW=40:SH=24:
      KZ=-16384:KW=-16368:RETURN
970   WU=50:RETURN
```

The program will run as is on the Apple II+ and IIe. See the Reference Manual, page 122, for changes for all other computers.

"Uh-oh," you mutter. "I knew that seemed too easy. I can see from the listing that you need a password to get into the system, but this program is rigged so that it is impossible to enter the password. All I get is an ominous message: 'So long, buddy.' "

"Uh-oh," Dutch echoes. "We've got problems. This thing is booby-trapped. There's a bomb in here. Well, that's my specialty. I can disarm anything — if I have the time. How long do I have, Orion?"

"I don't know. Until I can get into the system, I can't tell you a thing. But 'So long, buddy' kind of makes me think you'd better hurry." You swallow hard. There's got to be a way of slowing down the program to give you enough time to enter the password. But how?

"Countess, you'd better leave now," Dutch says.

"What? And leave my teammates?" the Countess answers in her best Transylvanian accent.

Suddenly, you get an idea. "I think I can do it," you say in a tiny voice, as your hands go to the keyboard again.

List the program and study it. Find the password. Then see if you can change the program to give you a bit more time to enter the password. Run the program. Good luck. You'll have to enter the password very quickly or it won't work. If you're stumped, consult the Reference Manual, page 121.

"You did it!" The Countess pounds your back enthusiastically.

"A good thing, too," Dutch says calmly. "There's enough plastic explosive here to blow a hole big enough to bury the Washington Monument."

That was one piece of information you could have done without. "Countess, will you pass me a towel, please?" Your T-shirt, fresh not 20 minutes ago, is soaking wet. After drying off, you get down to business, ready to examine the system. But the listings are too complicated to understand without a great deal of study.

"This will take too long," you tell them. "Dutch, can you rig him so when he's activated, he can talk but not get up?"

"Sure." He unplugs a pair of cables. "He — it's — all yours."

"Okay, AS-1, what are your orders?" you ask.

In a toneless voice, AS-1 responds, "First, find the young person who entered the estate with Agent Scott and bring same to headquarters."

"Where's headquarters?" Dutch says.

"The computer building."

"Why did they want me there?" you continue your questioning.

"I do not know."

"Okay. Then what?"

There is a pause. "That does not compute," he responds.

"What other orders have you been given?"

"I am to keep close to the President." The Countess's breath whistles between her teeth. In all the excitement you had forgotten that she hadn't been briefed about the mission. She doesn't know the President is in danger. "Accompany him to the circus tonight. When the lights go out, immobilize him."

"How?" the Countess demands, fists propped on her broad hips.

"There is a capsule I am to break under his nose."

Dutch frowns. "What's in the capsule?"

"Benylataladigitin."

"Oh, dear heaven," the Countess says softly.

Dutch looks up at her. "You know something about this stuff?"

"It's a lethal gas. Half a whiff and you're in a coma for life. A whole whiff and it causes a massive heart attack."

Dutch's eyes widen to saucer size. "How do you know? That don't sound like the kind of thing you'd use in a circus!"

The Countess flushes and clears her throat. "Okay, listen. I'm FBI. I do a bit of counter-espionage work here and there, and that's how I know Macklin. Now I'd appreciate it if you'd forget I told you that, both of you. What are we going to do? Why do they want to kill the President?"

AS-1 assumes she's talking to him. "So that VL-2 can take his place," he drones.

"Who the heck is VL-2?" Dutch asks in confusion.

"I do not know," the android responds obediently.

In that instant you get the whole picture: "VL — Vincent Loggins, the Vice-President," you gasp. "But not the real one — a Vice-President diordna. I saw it! It was plugged in and ready to go. AS-1, how many are there of you? How many diordnas?"

"Seventeen have been activated, four are in charge, twelve are in storage and will not be formatted until they are needed."

"Those are mighty big odds," Dutch mutters uncomfortably. "It's gonna take one heck of a plan to stop these boys."

"I want to know once and for all who these 'boys' are," you tell him. "Who gives you your orders, AS-1?"

Suddenly, he seems to have short-circuited again. "A-blee, a-bl-blee, a-blee," he babbles, sounding like Porky Pig.

"He can't tell us. He's programmed not to respond."

"Try a 'yes' or 'no' question," the Countess says. "And toss that Eturbee person at him, that name I keep sensing in connection with this whole business. It's stronger now than it was yesterday."

You turn to stare at her, the answer to a puzzle beginning to surface. "Countess, how do you spell that?"

She closes her eyes, as if she's reading the insides of her eyelids. "E-T-U-R-B-E-E. It's a very unusual name."

"You've almost got it," you inform her. "It's BRUTE!"

AS-1 sits bolt upright. His hand jerks to his temple in a snappy salute. "BRUTE forever! We are all instruments of BRUTE!! AS-1 ready to receive your orders!"

Dutch wears a grin wide enough to split his face in two. "Well, well, well. Looks like you hit the nail smack on the head, Orion. He's BRUTE's boy. So what shall we tell this bozo to do?"

You toss around a couple of ideas in your head, but none of them seems quite the right answer. "We need to find Scotty. AS-1, where is Agent Scott?"

"Headquarters. I am ready to receive your orders," he reminds you.

"We'll leave him here for now," you decide. You push the button in his abdomen and he slumps forward. "Countess, you're officially on the team now. And, Dutch, I guess you're team coordinator for the time being."

"No way." He shakes his head adamantly. "We're all in the same boat and on equal terms until we find the boss. We know where he is, so let's go get him."

"But the President," the Countess says. "We have to warn him not to go to the circus tonight. I'll go talk to him if you like."

Dutch clears his throat. "Countess, no disrespect intended, but if you go marching up there in your red robes and ostrich plumes, they're going to lock you up as one of those loonies, and ask their questions later. And if it's one of these diordna fellows, he won't even bother with the questions. He'll just bash you over the head and stow you somewhere."

The Countess looks insulted for half a second, then shrugs. "You're right."

"I guess I should do it," you tell them. "I met him once. He might even remember."

"Terrific!" Dutch says. "We'll wait outside for you. If you aren't back within 10 minutes, we'll come in after you."

"Sure, and get your head blown off by an agent doing his job, or a diordna following BRUTE's orders. No, if I don't come out, find Scotty. After the President, he's the second most important person to get to."

With those words ringing in your ears, you head for the castle and the President.

CHAPTER
7

The walk across the drawbridge feels like the longest you've ever taken. Lifting a knocker the size of a meat platter, you bang on the door. After an eternity, it's opened by a tall, skinny man in a black suit who looks as if he should be the host of a haunted house. His deep-set eyes stare down at you. "What do you want?" he demands. "You don't belong here." His face doesn't look quite real. It's very pale and his skin looks loose. There's something familiar about his voice.

"I've got to see the President," you announce as firmly as you can.

"You know that's impossible," he answers.

"I've got to see him. It's a matter of life and death!"

He leans down, peers into your face, and

his pupils flare oddly. He straightens up. "Come in. I will ask him, but he does not feel well."

"I promise it won't take long."

He turns, looks back at you one last time, then leaves by a door on the right. You are left standing in a great, cavernous hall.

In a few moments, the door opens and the President strides in, the same President you remember with his enormous feet and friendly blue eyes. Only they don't look quite as friendly as you hoped. There's something else about them that bothers you, but you can't put your finger on it. And it's obvious he doesn't remember you. *Of course he doesn't,* you say to yourself.

He coughs. "You wanted to see me? Pardon me if I ask you not to keep me too long. My stomach seems to be upset. I was just about to go to bed."

"You aren't going to the circus?" you ask, your spirits lifting.

"I'm afraid not. I hate to disappoint them, but I just don't feel well enough."

"Promise me you won't go, Mr. President, even if you feel better later. Your life is in danger if you do."

His bushy eyebrows lift. "Oh?"

You're just about to explain when you see a long shadow just inside the door through which the President came. There's no way you're going to tell your story with that guy hanging around. "It's too complicated to go into right now. But everything will be all right if you stay away from the circus," you tell him, lowering your voice to a whisper.

He gives you a sad smile. "In that case, you have nothing to worry about. I'll be in bed the rest of the day and probably won't get up until tomorrow. But you must come back and tell me what is going on."

"I will, sir, I promise. I hope you feel better."

He puts a hand to his stomach. "I'm sure I will. Thank you for your concern." He walks with you to the door and lets you out.

The Countess and Dutch appear from under the edge of the drawbridge where they were hiding. "He's not going tonight," you announce. "He's sick. If we can find Scotty, maybe he can keep an eye on him for the rest of the day."

"What did he say about all those androids walking around?" Dutch asks.

"I didn't tell him. A real creep of a guy was hanging around, and I didn't want him to hear. The President asked me to come back and fill him in. I said I would, since he really didn't look quite right."

Dutch shrugs. "Well, I guess that was all you could do. So let's go see if we can find the boss."

The Countess seems a bit distracted as the three of you round the castle and head for the computer building, keeping under cover of the trees.

"Something wrong?" Dutch asks her.

She shudders, as if hit with a sudden chill. "There is great evil in that building. We must be careful."

If being warned was supposed to make you feel any better, something went wrong. You were edgy before — now you're downright scared.

Inside the computer complex, you cross to the elevators. "They probably have Scotty stashed in the subbasement. The only problem is, I'm not sure how I got down there. The elevator's computerized —" You stop, a sheepish smile on your face.

Dutch attacks the control panel with a screwdriver and opens it up. Inside is a small, no-frills terminal. Connecting your portable to it so you can use your own display screen, you bring up the program that moves the elevator.

Input the program and list it. Lines 150 and 960 must each be typed as one line.

PROGRAM 5

```
100  REM  ELEVATOR
110  GOSUB 960:GOSUB 970
120  GOSUB 900
130  PRINT "ENTER CODE ";:INPUT KD$
140  IF KD$="7235" THEN 170
```

```
150   IF KD$="5327" THEN A=1:
      B=SH-8:C=1:GOTO 180
160   GOTO 120
170   A=SH-8:B=1:C=-1
180   GOSUB 900
190   TL$="   !   ":T$="+--!--+"
200   SD$="!     !":B$="+-----+"
210   BL$="      "
220   HT=INT(SW/4)
230   FOR VT=1 TO A
240   GOSUB 910:PRINT TL$
250   NEXT VT
260   VT=A
270   GOSUB 910:PRINT TL$:VT=VT+1
280   GOSUB 910:PRINT T$:VT=VT+1
290   FOR I=1 TO 3
300   GOSUB 910:PRINT SD$
310   VT=VT+1
320   NEXT I
330   GOSUB 910:PRINT B$:VT=VT+1
340   GOSUB 910:PRINT BL$
350   REM  MOVE ELEVATOR
360   FOR I=A TO B STEP C
370   GOSUB 400
380   NEXT I
390   END
400   VT=I:GOSUB 910
410   PRINT TL$:VT=VT+1
420   GOSUB 910:PRINT T$
430   VT=VT+1:GOSUB 910:PRINT SD$
440   VT=I+5:GOSUB 910:PRINT SD$
450   VT=VT+1:GOSUB 910:PRINT B$
460   VT=VT+1:GOSUB 910:PRINT BL$
```

```
470   WT=WU:GOSUB 920
480   RETURN
900   HOME:RETURN
910   VTAB(VT):HTAB(HT):RETURN
920   FOR WS=1 TO WT:NEXT WS
960   NU$=CHR$(Ø):SW=4Ø:SH=24:
      KZ=-16384:KW=-16368:RETURN
970   WU=3Ø:RETURN
```

The program will run as is on the Apple II+ and IIe. See the Reference Manual, page 124, for changes for all other computers.

You expect to find the 3–2–7–5 code in the listing, but it isn't there. Has someone changed the code already?

A closer look brings a smile of relief to your face. You can find the new codes that will move the elevator.

Can you figure out how to make the elevator go down to the subbasement? Study the program to find the new codes. Then run the program to make the elevator go up and down. If you're having trouble, consult the Reference Manual, page 123.

The elevator drops smoothly to the sub-basement. The hall is empty, silent. "This way," you whisper and trot toward the sixth door.

Just as you're about to insert your badge into the reader, Dutch stops you. "Countess, you sense anybody in there?"

Her eyes narrow. You can almost see her invisible antennae at work. "Scotty's there," she whispers. "His aura's very weak. But remember, androids have no auras. If there are any in there with him, I wouldn't be able to tell."

"It's a chance we'll have to take," Dutch replies firmly. "Okay, Orion, use your badge."

The door glides open. Dutch sticks his head in, then nods. "All clear. And here's our boy."

Scotty is stretched out on one of the tables, a small mask over his nose. The mask is connected by a clear, plastic tube to a tall, red cylinder near his head. A second table is also occupied by a body that is completely covered by a sheet. You lift one end of it. It's the same android you saw before, the Vice-President's double.

The Countess crosses to the cylinder and peers at the label on it. "These people are not nice at all," she growls, as she closes the valve on the cylinder and removes the mask. "This combination of gases slows your heart and rate of respiration and then causes your temperature to drop." She places her hand against his cheek. "He's colder than a TV dinner."

"At least he's alive," Dutch says, reaching for the straps across Scotty's chest.

The Countess's head snaps up. "Someone is coming this way," she hisses. "It's the evil one. What are we going to do?"

"Hide," Dutch says tersely, crossing to the bank of lockers against the wall. He opens one; it is occupied by a diordna. He opens the next two. They are empty. "Countess, Orion, women and children first."

"Sorry, Dutch," the Countess responds. "I suffer from claustrophobia. Ten seconds in a space that small and I'd go bonkers. Here." She snatches the sheet from the Vice-President diordna. "Put him in there, and I'll take his place."

Dutch helps stand the android upright and they carry him to the locker and stuff him in. Meanwhile, you check the lockers at the other end to find a vacant one for Dutch. The first one is occupied, and opening the second, you come face-to-face with yourself! The blood drains from your head and you slump against the door. The diordna looks just like you!

Dutch closes the locker on the Vice-President and comes to see what's wrong. He looks at it, then at you. "Wow! It's a dead ringer, Orion." He opens the third locker. "Empty. Get in there before you faint."

The last thing you see as he closes the door on you is the Countess on the table, covering herself with the sheet. If you stand on your toes, you can see out of the louvers. The Countess makes a credible android, except for the sweep of three ostrich plumes that stick out beyond the sheet.

"Psst, Countess, your feathers!" you hiss.

A hand comes up and plucks them out of sight. Suddenly, you freeze with terror. Dutch must not have closed the locker door securely, because ever so slowly, it begins to swing open. It stops when it's halfway open. Closing it now would make too much noise.

Your attention shifts to the intruder and you almost pass out again. It's easy to recognize the formal black suit and stiff white collar worn by the old geezer who let you into the castle. But as he turns to speak to the man with him, he pulls at the skin under his chin, peels off his face, and stuffs it in his pocket. No wonder he seemed familiar! It's your old enemy, Dr. Arsene, who almost fed you to the wolves in Solonia! So *he* is the link with BRUTE!

He removes the clipboard from its hanger and checks it. "Very good." The sound of his voice, undisguised now, raises goosebumps the size of Ping-Pong balls on your arms. "We have very few left to capture. Once we've eliminated the President and replaced him with our friend here'' — he pats the lump under the sheet — ''we can signal our man in Moscow to take care of the Premier over there. Then at the summit meeting, with BRUTE's diordnas substituted for all the world leaders, our plan for domination of this planet will at last be in effect.''

''What about Senator Macklin, sir?'' the man with him asks. You look at him for the first time: Agent Grantly, who'd tried to get on the elevator with you. ''He sent the ACT team here. He's bound to make trouble.''

Arsene scowls. ''Yes. We will have to eliminate the Senator immediately — and the fat lady. Access to the Net makes it very easy to keep tabs on everyone in their government,'' he says coolly.

''What will we do with the diordna we were to format as the Senator?''

Arsene turns to check on Scotty. ''We'll use it for the guard at the front gates. While the circus is performing, you immobilize him and put him in the duplicator.''

His bony face stretches in an evil smile. ''I must say that putting the duplicator at the front gate has worked out. Not one person has suspected it is not just a security device.''

The door opens and someone you cannot see says, ''AS-1 is nowhere to be found, sir. And your orders to capture the teenager did not reach us in time. But we are searching the grounds.''

"Find AS-1 and that kid or you will be deactivated permanently!" Dr. Arsene snarls. The door closes. "In the meantime, DG-4, we will ready the diordna of that agent. Place the android here." He nods toward an empty table as he reaches to take Scotty's pulse.

Before you have time to panic, the door of your locker opens wide. DG-4 reaches in and grabs your upper arms as if he's lifting a doll. There's nothing you can do except hold yourself as rigid as possible. That's easy enough — you're scared stiff!

DG-4 places you on the table and moves away. Dr. Arsene turns to reach for a cable from one of the monitors near your head. Your brain reels with terror. What will he do when he doesn't find a socket to plug that thing into?

"Perfect, perfect," the doctor murmurs as he rolls up your sleeve. Then he is the one to freeze with surprise. "This is no android!"

Suddenly the room comes alive! The Countess sits up straight, tossing back the sheet. "Call me a fat lady, will you?" She launches herself toward Dr. Arsene. You have to give the old buzzard credit — he's fast. In an instant, he has whipped out a gun from somewhere, and you just know the Countess is going to die. She is saved, however, when her legs are snarled by the sheet and she falls beside the table. As she goes down, one of her flailing arms knocks the gun from Arsene's hand. He heads for the door.

In the meantime, Dutch comes flying out of his locker. He hesitates, focused on DG-4, then apparently decides the doctor's more important. "I'll get him!" he shouts, and hurtles toward the door where Dr. Arsene is struggling to get his badge into the card reader.

The Countess, not to be outdone, jumps to her feet. Just as DG-4 reaches for his own gun, she gives him a belt in the midsection that lifts him off his feet. Bent double, he bounces off the lockers and tilts over, ending up with his forehead against the cold tile floor, his rear end in the air. He looks like an upside down V, and it's obvious he's not going anywhere.

Dr. Arsene, seeing Dutch barreling toward him, sidesteps him neatly and heads in your direction. Opening the valve on the gas cylinder beside your table with one hand and grabbing the hose with the other, you take aim for the doctor's face. He is unable to check his forward motion to avoid you. A ferocious hissing fills the air and the good doctor slowly slumps to the floor.

"We did it!" The Countess is dancing with glee. " 'Fat lady,' indeed!"

Dutch grins. "That was close, wasn't it? Look, let's put the old dude on a table, strap him down, and give him more of his own medicine. We need to keep him out of our hair for a while." That takes less than a minute, because Dr. Arsene doesn't weigh very much. "Now, how are we going to carry Scotty?"

"No sweat," the Countess says. "The fat lady, I'm not; the strong lady, I am." Pulling Scotty into a sitting position, she stoops, drapes him over her shoulder, and pushes herself upright. "Let's get out of here."

But you are not home free quite yet. At the elevator, you hear shouts from above. "Darn," Dutch says, "somebody — or something's — in the lobby. We can't go up. Guess we'll have to hide until the coast is clear. Come on."

He sets off toward the left. The Countess follows, carrying Scotty with ease, and you bring up the rear.

"Uh-oh," Dutch grunts. "I hear footsteps up ahead. This way." He darts into a short hallway that shoots off on the right. There are two doors in this alcove, one facing the other, both locked. "In the corner. Maybe they'll go by so fast they won't see us."

"Better be prepared in case they do," the Countess whispers. She lowers Scotty, stands him on his feet against the dead-end wall, and plants a big hand against his chest to pin him there — and almost falls over herself as Scotty's end of the wall moves backward. It swivels on a pivot in the center, and Scotty tumbles backward through the opening into darkness. Then the wall swings back into place.

The three of you stare at it in shock. You recover first. "Let's see what's back there." A gentle pressure against it and it swings open again. You almost fall over Scotty. The Countess, behind you, nudges him out of the way so Dutch can get through, then picks him up again. He groans softly.

"This must lead somewhere," Dutch says. "We might as well find out where."

For the first few yards, you follow one another, hand on the shoulder of the one in front, groping your way. But after a short distance, your eyes adjust and you realize that there is a dim light. This hall, or tunnel, or whatever it is, is a very long, steep, uphill climb. The Countess begins to stagger.

"Want to stop and rest?" you ask.

"I'll try carrying him," Dutch volunteers.

She says, "No. It's not that bad."

But it's another 10 minutes of uphill going before you see the end of the road, in this case another blank wall. Dutch runs ahead and pushes on one end of it. Just as the other did, it swings open on a pivot, and after a nod from him that it's okay, the three of you step through into the rear of a closet as large as a small room. Suits line one wall, sweaters and shirts a second, and shoes a third.

"We must be in the castle," you offer. You tiptoe to the door opposite the pivoting wall and listen. Nothing. Opening it cautiously, you peek out. It's an enormous bedroom, a huge four-poster bed in the center. There's no one in sight. "Okay," you whisper, opening the door wide so the Countess can get through.

She is winded now, perspiration streaming down her face. She heads straight for the four-poster and dumps her burden. As soon as Scotty's head hits the soft, velvet spread, he opens his mouth and begins to snore so loudly, the three of you look at him in horror.

"Well, what have we here?" a familiar voice asks. You spin around and there stands the President in a doorway you simply hadn't had time to notice. He waits for someone to speak, his bushy brows raised with curiosity.

He crosses to Dutch. "You must be the ACT team. Macklin briefed me. Don't think I've had the pleasure. Jason McNally." He shakes Dutch's hand.

Dutch clears his throat. "Wilhelm Haas, Mr. President. Just call me Dutch."

"And you." The famous blue eyes turn in your direction. "We've met. I never forget a face. Ah, yes, in the White House. A class trip, wasn't it? I hope you appreciated how clever my remarks were to you. It was the best I could do to indicate that I knew of your association with ACT." He grins wickedly, his eyes sparkle, and finally you pinpoint what had bothered you downstairs: The tiny streaks of hazel in his eyes were missing before. You'd once had a cat with eyes like that, and when you'd met the President last year, he'd reminded you of Catwallader. But earlier today, the man you spoke to had plain blue eyes. You must have been talking to an android!

CHAPTER
8

After the President has introduced himself to the Countess, he settles into a chair and asks, "Now what have you good folks done to Agent Scott here?"

"Oh, goodness! Scotty!" The Countess goes to the bed and checks his temperature. "He's still not up to normal, but his snoring is a good sign. We should get something hot into him." She pulls up the edges of the spread and wraps him in it. "That should help, too."

"I'll ring for a pot of coffee," the President offers.

"Uh — that's fine, sir," Dutch says, "but don't count on the old guy in the black suit. We had to put him out of action for the time being. He's with BRUTE!"

"Andrews? With BRUTE? That's impossible. He's been with me for years!"

"I'm sorry, Mr. President," Dutch begins. "The man you thought was your valet isn't really Andrews. He's actually Arsene, a BRUTE operative. Obviously his disguise was good enough to fool even you!"

The coffee arrives, and then you and Dutch brief the President on everything that has happened so far.

The Countess, who is pouring hot coffee into Scotty, adds a comment to the recital of events every now and then.

"And they made a double for me, too?" the President asks. "I wonder how. I didn't go through their miracle copier at the gate. And if BRUTE intends to kill me and substitute an android of Vince Loggins, they must not plan to use mine."

"I think I know why," you volunteer. "It's the eyes. They did a pretty good job on it, but they didn't get the little brown flecks in your eyes."

"But still, it was good enough to fool you when you came here before," he reminds you.

"Yes, but there was something about you — it — that bothered me. There was so much going on, though, that I didn't have time to figure it out. I just knew it was something about the eyes." You stop there, not daring to admit he reminded you of your Siamese cat when you'd met him last year.

"And they got Vince," he says sadly.

"And my cabinet. All those fine people. . . ."

"Nodded," Scotty mumbles. "Frome."

Dutch frowns. "What was that?"

The agent shudders and opens his eyes blearily. It's a tremendous effort for him to talk. "Not dead," he says with an obvious effort to speak clearly. "Frozen. Room in subbasement back of where you found me."

"Did you know about the subbasement, Mr. President?" Dutch asks.

He nods. "Of course. It's Castleman's bomb shelter. BRUTE must have found out about it and decided to use it for their own purposes. Now, what are we going to do about this?"

"No 'we,' "Dutch says. "Just us four. The whole point of ACT becoming involved was to see that no harm came to you."

"Right," Scotty manages as firmly as he can. "No more," he groans as the Countess refills his cup.

"Drink up, Scotty," the President directs. "We need you alert and thinking. It seems to me that if you've already taken care of this Arsene character, the next order of business is to do something about those androids. I must say I'm a bit unsettled at the thought of them all walking around this estate, wearing the faces of my friends and colleagues. The problem is what to do. You can't go around poking everyone in the belly button!''

"Couldn't anyway," Scotty says. He looks a little green in the face, but sits up straight and tries to look alert. "Arsene did a lot of gloating before he put me under, and one of the things he mentioned was that the androids are programmed to protect their midsections."

"Well, I'll certainly cancel the circus," President McNally says. "And I'll have the National Guard here and — "

"Mr. President, I don't think we can proceed that way," Scotty says, suddenly much stronger. "First, there isn't time. Secondly, keeping the security lid on this will be impossible if you bring in the military."

The President nods his agreement. A heavy silence hangs over the group. Finally Dutch says, "All those androids in one place — it gives me the creeps."

"Wait a minute." You hop to your feet and begin pacing the floor. "It seems to me that's exactly what we do want — all of them in one place, I mean."

"What good would that do?" the Countess asks.

You reach your hand into your pocket and pull out your miniature computer. "Maybe I can use this to alter the androids' programming. Maybe we can turn their invention against their creators."

"No, it would take too long to reprogram

92

each android," Scotty says. "But you've given me the beginning of an idea." Scotty's still shivering, but he's obviously taken charge of the mission again. "Dutch, is there some way to radio orders to those things, those androids?"

"Just simple stuff. You can't order them to self-destruct or anything like that," Dutch replies.

"But could you order them to come to the circus tonight?" Scotty asks a bit impatiently.

"With a little luck — if I get the right frequency — yeah, I guess I could."

"Well, do it!" Scotty barks. Then in a more mellow tone of voice, he says, "Mr. President, promise me you won't attend tonight's performance of the circus."

President McNally gives a grudging nod. "You have my word. And I'll be waiting to hear from you."

Scotty rises from the bed, stands a moment as if to be sure of his balance, and walks unsteadily toward the door.

"Where are we going?" you ask, since he doesn't look as if he'd get very far.

"To find the President's android. Arsene may not have plans for it, but I do. And we'll need to stop at your cabin and pick up my double, since he — I mean it — was supposed to be the official escort." After a second's hesitation, he asks, "Does anybody have a gun? I seem to have been relieved of mine."

Dutch reaches behind his back and removes a nasty-looking automatic from his belt. "This was Dr. Arsene's."

"Leave it here," Scotty instructs. "Just in case you need it, Mr. President." He opens the bedroom door before turning to deliver one last word. "When we come back to report in to you, sir, the first thing we'll do is let you give us a poke below the belt as proof that we're us."

"Just a minute," the Countess begins, then changes her mind. "Well, I guess it will be all right, this once."

The President grins broadly. "I'll look forward to it, Countess," he says, bowing at the waist gallantly.

CHAPTER
9

It takes half an hour of searching to find the President's android. Mr. Castleman does indeed have a dungeon — several of them, in fact — and the android was stashed in the darkest corner of one. Fortunately, since you know the password and don't have to worry about the thing blowing everything to smithereens, altering its programming to obey your commands doesn't take very long. So the four of you and "it" return to your cabin to put AS-1 back in operation.

Scotty takes one look at his double and breaks out in a cold sweat. "Great guns, he — it — gives me the creeps! It does look like me, doesn't it?"

"Nonsense!" the Countess says huffily. "It's nowhere near as handsome. So, what's our plan?"

Turning his back on his twin, Scotty scrubs a freckled hand over his face. "It's not much of a plan, really. But we've got to get rid of the androids. So, why not follow the script Arsene had written? It's as good as any. The lights go out, but instead of AS-1 breaking a capsule under the President's nose, which wouldn't do any good anyhow, considering our pal there doesn't have a working nose, what if AS-1 puts all the androids out of action with his trusty peashooter?"

"All of them? All by himself?"

"He might be able to do it, Scotty," you offer. "Those diordnas can move so fast, all you see is a blur. If we could get the rest of the people out of the way, maybe when the lights go out, I could program him to get up with his gun drawn, and then just swing around in an arc, firing."

"But how do we get the people out of the way so no one gets hurt?" the Countess asks. "How's AS-1 supposed to tell us from them, Orion?"

"Uh — gee, I don't know. He sure wouldn't be able to tell just by looking. The only reason I realized AS-1 wasn't Scotty was because he didn't have the cut on his finger."

"It's a shame he doesn't have X-ray eyes," Dutch remarks.

"Wait a minute," you cry as a lightbulb glows in your head. "He doesn't have X-ray eyes, but he does have a hearing mechanism

96

so sensitive he can hear a gnat sneeze at the other end of a football field."

"So?" Dutch asks.

"He can hear heartbeats! All I have to do is rewrite his orders so that he shoots only if he doesn't hear a heartbeat."

"Orion, you are brilliant!" the Countess shouts. "That's a terrific idea!"

You grin. "It is, isn't it?" Turning back to AS-1, you put the terrific idea into action. "He's ready," you say, as you push his ON button. Slowly, he comes to life, blinking rapidly.

Scotty steps in front of him. "How you doing, son?" he asks expansively.

"Fine, thank you, sir," AS-1 responds hoarsely.

"What gives?" Dutch asks. "He catching a cold? Good grief, what am I saying?"

"Probably water damage to his throat box," you respond. "He spent a few minutes in the shower stall with the spray on full blast."

"What difference does it make?" Scotty asks. "We're not asking him to sing, just to shoot straight. Let's get out of here. He makes me nervous." He crosses to the door and beckons to his double, who stands watching, his head tilted to one side as if he isn't quite sure who Scotty is. "What are you waiting for? We're on our way to the circus, man. Do your job."

AS-1 walks to the corner where the Presidential android has been sitting quietly. You'd almost forgotten he was there. "Mr. President," AS-1 murmurs respectfully.

"Ah, yes, Agent Scott," the President's double replies, getting to his feet. "Are we ready to go?"

"I don't believe this," Scotty mumbles, opening the door for them. "This is truly creepy."

"They should go first," Dutch says. "You'll need to keep out of sight. It'll ruin everything if you and AS-1 are seen together."

"Fine by me," Scotty growls, watching the two androids stride toward the entertainment complex.

At the amphitheater, the audience is smaller than you'd expected, perhaps 20 people. "Not many here," you remark to Scotty.

"Most are coming to tomorrow's performance — if there is one. It's just as well. The fewer around, the fewer to get hurt."

You and your teammates are standing in the dark behind the last row of seats. Below you, on stage, a pair of riggers are checking the wire-walker's equipment, and some clowns are adjusting the tension on a trampoline. Over to your right, the Presidential android and AS-1 have stopped at the top of the stairs leading down to the seats and seem to be having a pleasant chat. It's eerie watching them. They look so normal, AS-1 tilting his head to the right as if to catch every word being said. He sees you, and crosses to your side.

"What's up?" Scotty asks, stepping deeper into the shadows.

"There's a problem, sir," the Scotty android tells you. "If I am to shoot everyone here, I must have more ammunition. And from whom shall I take my orders after I shoot you?"

"Shoot me?" you squeak. "What are you talking about? I'm no android!"

"But you have no heartbeat."

Your hand flies to your chest before you can stop yourself. "That's ridiculous! Of course, I have a —" Your protest trails off as what AS-1 said finally registers. "Shoot *everyone* here?"

"Those were your orders. No one here has a heartbeat. I must shoot them all, if I can."

Belatedly, you notice how AS-1 is looking at you, the way he keeps tilting his head to one side, a slight frown on his face. "It's his ears," you murmur. "He must have water in his receivers. That's why he's been holding his head that way."

Dutch gapes at AS-1. "His supersensitive hearing is on the fritz? Boy, are we in trouble now!"

At that moment, there's a strange hissing in the earpiece of your communicator. "How sad," a dry, rasping voice whispers, and you freeze. It's Dr. Arsene! "Yes, I escaped, since you failed to check if there were any other androids in the building. One came to my aid."

"Got to find him," Scotty says, and takes off running with Dutch right behind him.

"Don't bother, Mr. Scott," the doctor's voice grates. "I'm too far away for you to catch me in time. Had things gone as I'd planned, only one person would have died here tonight: your beloved President McNally. But because of your meddling, I've changed all that. Now everyone here will die."

"You're bluffing," Dutch spits into his communicator.

"Am I? Each of the androids contains a plastic explosive, originally intended as a booby trap to prevent interference with their programming. But I have made a very small alteration so that they will explode when I, from my remote location, use their own circuitry to send a small charge of electricity through the plastic." You gasp with horror. How can you stop him?

"Such marvelous goo," he continues. "Hit it, throw it, nothing happens. But one spark of current and, ah, the carnage!" You can hear the delight in his voice. "I may do it any time I like, perhaps a minute from now, or two minutes. . . ."

Despite the chaos raging in your mind, you realize that something must be done, and you're the one who'll have to do it — now. You'll have to put those androids out of commission immediately, so that Dr. Arsene's signal to generate that charge of electricity will be sent to carcasses full of smoking wires and ruined circuitry, courtesy of a bullet from AS-1's gun. If Scotty or Dutch will just keep him talking, keep him bragging. . . .

Hurriedly you go into the programming you had written and delete the commands for the android to wait for the blackout and to shoot at anyone without a heartbeat.

"What are you doing?" the Countess asks.

But you're too busy to answer. As rapidly as your trembling fingers will permit, you type in changes.

When you've finished, Dr. Arsene is still rattling on about his plans for world domination. Ripping off the microphone of your communicator, you toss it on the floor and stomp on it, gesturing for the Countess to do the same.

She removes hers and grinds it into pieces under her heel. "Why are we doing this?" she whispers.

"So Dr. Arsene won't hear us or anything that's happening here." Then at the top of your lungs, you yell, "BRUTE SAYS: ATTEN-TION!!" Immediately, all the Secret Service agents and the Vice-President stand rigidly, chests out, chins back, hands to their foreheads in a snappy salute. There are at least 20 of them and they stand out like sore thumbs. But this is no time to congratulate yourself. You're not finished.

"HIT THE DIRT, EVERYONE!!" you scream, as you type in RUN. The androids do not move. After all, you didn't say "BRUTE says. . . ."

The Countess, bless her ostrich plumes, gets the idea immediately and yells, "HEY RUBE!!" a warning used by circus and carnival people. "EVERYONE DOWN!!" Those you can see hesitate for a fraction of a second and then throw themselves to the ground. The men in the audience look around in confusion, some rising from their seats. The Countess waves for them to duck.

But your focus is on AS-1. You'd programmed him to station himself at the top of the bank of seats, draw his weapon, and begin shooting in a wide arc, all at triple speed.

But something is wrong! AS-1 isn't responding. His head still tilted to one side, he has moved to the top of the center aisle, but nowhere near as fast as you'd expected. He pulls out his weapon and swings it in a wide arc. But he does not fire!

"What's he waiting for?" the Countess says.

"We dried out his microprocessor," you explain, "but we didn't think about water damage to the rest of his circuitry."

So, again, it's up to you. You'll have to make the moves for AS-1, aim his weapon, and fire it. You can only hope to destroy all the androids before Dr. Arsene realizes what's going on.

Input the following program and run it. Lines 320, 350, 480, 520, 530, 540, 560, 940, 950, and 960 must each be typed as one line. Hit the "F" key to fire AS-1's gun for him. Plan your shots carefully, or you'll run out of bullets.

PROGRAM 6

```
100  REM SHOOT-OUT
110  DIM R(50),RV(50),RH(50)
120  NR=20:NB=20
130  GOSUB 960:GOSUB 970
140  GOSUB 900
150  GOSUB 450
160  FOR I=1 TO 4
170  READ J1,J2,J3,J4,J5,J6
180  DH(I)=J1:DV(I)=J2:QH(I)=J3:
     QV(I)=J4:SF(I)=J5:EF(I)=J6
190  IF QH(I)=2 THEN QH(I)=SW
200  IF QV(I)=2 THEN QV(I)=SH-1
210  IF SF(I)=8 THEN SF(I)=SH-2
220  IF SF(I)=9 THEN SF(I)=SW
230  IF EF(I)=8 THEN EF(I)=SH-2
240  IF EF(I)=9 THEN EF(I)=SW
250  NEXT I
260  VP=1
270  HP=1
280  I=1
290  VT=VP:HT=HP:GOSUB 910:PRINT " ";
300  VP=VP+DV(I):HP=HP+DH(I)
310  VT=VP:HT=HP:GOSUB 910:PRINT "O";
320  IF ((VP=QV(I))*(HP=QH(I))) THEN
     I=I+1:IF I=5 THEN I=1
```

103

```
330    GOSUB 940:IF KY$<>"F" THEN 440
340    FV=VP+DH(I):FH=HP-DV(I)
350    SS=INT((EF(I)-SF(I)))/
       ABS(INT((EF(I) - SF(I))))
360    FOR J=SF(I)+SS TO EF(I) STEP SS
370    VT=FV:HT=FH:GOSUB 910:PRINT " ";
380    FV=FV+DH(I):FH=FH-DV(I)
390    VT=FV:HT=FH
400    GOSUB 910:PRINT "*";
410    NEXT J
420    GOSUB 910:PRINT " ";
430    GOSUB 510
440    GOTO 290
450    FOR I=1 TO NR
460    RX=SW-3:GOSUB 930:RH(I)=RD+1
470    RX=SH-3:GOSUB 930:RV(I)=RD+1
480    VT=RV(I):HT=RH(I):GOSUB 910
       :PRINT "R";
490    NEXT I
500    RETURN
510    FOR R=1 TO NR
520    IF DV(I)<>0 THEN IF RV(R)=VP
       THEN RK=RK+ 1:RH(R)=0:RV(R)=0
530    IF DH(I)<>0 THEN IF RH(R)=HP
       THEN RK=RK+ 1:RH(R)=0:RV(R)=0
540    IF RK=NR THEN GOSUB 900:PRINT
       "YOU WIN!!":END
550    NEXT R
560    NF=NF+1:IF NF>NB THEN GOSUB
       900:PRINT "NO MORE BULLETS":END
570    RETURN
580    DATA 1,0,2,1,2,8,0,1,2,2,9,2
590    DATA -1,0,1,2,8,2,0,-1,1,1,2,9
```

```
800  XC$=MID$(A$,SB,SE):RETURN
820  A$=A$+B$:RETURN
900  HOME:RETURN
910  VTAB(VT):HTAB(HT):RETURN
930  RD=INT(RND(1)*RX)+1:RETURN
940  KY$=NU$:KY=PEEK(KZ)
     :IF KY<128 THEN RETURN
950  KY$=CHR$(KY-128):POKE KW,Ø
     :RETURN
960  NU$=CHR$(Ø):SW=4Ø:SH=24:
     KZ=-16384:KW=-16368:RETURN
970  RETURN
```

The program will run as is on the Apple II+ and IIe. See the Reference Manual, page 126, for changes for all other computers.

One by one, you hone in on each diordna and direct AS-1 to shoot. The amphitheater explodes in chaos, with circus performers scrambling to get out of the way. The air is acrid with the smell of gunpowder, and animals are screaming in terror behind the stage. From the corner of your eye, you see cabinet members and Presidential aides ducking beneath their seats. Their lives are in your hands and you concentrate on demolishing the androids as fast as you can.

As suddenly as it began, it's over. The silence is a surprise to the ears. The circus people come to life, checking on one another, and heads begin to peek up between the seats.

Scotty bolts up the stairs calling, ''Orion, you okay?''

You wave to indicate you're fine, getting a look at the destruction for the first time. It's unnerving. Bodies are strewn all over, wisps of smoke swirling from the gaping holes in their fronts. AS-1 is still frozen in position, the only android left.

Dutch runs over from the other side. ''Orion, you did it! 'BRUTE says, Attenshun!' Boy, they popped up like ducks in a shooting stand.''

''Anyone hurt?'' you ask, almost afraid to hear the answer.

''Not one,'' Dutch replies, softly. ''Not one.''

''What about Dr. Arsene?''

Scotty grimaces. ''Couldn't find him. I just hope he wasn't in the castle. I need to go check on the President.''

''Don't bother.'' You spin around to see the President approaching. ''I'm just fine. I see your plan worked. I figured I should be here to explain to the others. I want you to know I'm proud of all of you.''

''And I am so proud to have been a member of this team,'' the Countess says, ''and to have made a contribution to something so important. I'm almost sad it's over.''

You look down at the number of good, dedicated people the smoking androids represent, and leave it to Scotty to explain that as long as BRUTE and people like Dr. Arsene exist, the fight will never be over.

"You mean, you might be able to use me again?" the Countess asks.

"There's every possibility," Scotty says gently.

"Marvelous!" she bellows. "When you call, the Countess *(heavy accent)* and Myrtle Schwartz *(New Jersey all the way)* will be ready. In the meantime, shall we return to the castle? There's a small matter of belly buttons to attend to."

REFERENCE
MANUAL

Note to User: The programming activities in this book have been designed for use with the BASIC programming language on the IBM PC, PCjr, Apple II Plus or Apple IIe (with Applesoft BASIC), Commodore 64, VIC-20, Atari 400/800, Radio Shack TRS-80 Level 2 or greater, and the Radio Shack Color Computer. Each machine has its own operating procedures for starting up BASIC. So make sure you're in BASIC before trying to run any of these programs. Also make sure you type NEW before entering each program to clear out any leftovers from previous activities.

The version of the program included in the text will run as is on the Apple. You will have to modify the programs for the other computers. All the instructions you need are in this manual.

Even if you're using a computer other than the ones mentioned, the programs may still work, since they are always written in the most general BASIC.

If you need help with one of the computer activities in the *Micro Adventure,* or want to understand how a program works, you'll find what you need in this manual.

Naturally, programs must be typed into your computer *exactly* as given. If the program should run on your computer but you're having problems, do a list on the program and check your typing before you try anything else. Even a misplaced comma or space might cause an error of syntax that will prevent the whole program from working.

TERMS YOU NEED TO KNOW

Computer experts have a special "language" they use when talking about programs. Here are some common terms that will help you understand the explanations in this manual.

Arrays are groups of two or more logically related data elements in a program that have the same name. However, so that the individual elements in the array can be used, each is also identified by its own address (called an *index* by programmers). You can think of an array as an apartment building. One hundred people might live at the Northwest Apartments (or 100 pieces of information might be stored in the NW array). But each unit within the building has a number (like Apt 14), so that it can be located and receive mail. In the NW array, 14 could be the index to find a particular piece of information, and would be written NW (14). If you put the 26 letters of the alphabet into an array called Alpha, then Alpha (2) would equal B because B is the second letter of the alphabet.

ASCII (pronounced *asskee*) is the standard code used by most microcomputers to represent characters such as letters, numbers, and punctuation.

ASC is a function in BASIC that will supply a character's ASCII code. For example ASC ("A") will give you the number 65.

Bugs are errors or mistakes in a program that keep it from doing what it's supposed to do. Some of the programming activities in this book will ask you to find and fix a bug so that the program will work correctly.

Functions are ready-made routines that perform standard calculations in a program. It's sort of like having a key on a calculator that computes a square root or the cosine of a number. The programming language BASIC comes with a number of standard functions to perform certain tasks. For example, the function SQR(x) will find the square root of any number when x is replaced by that number. You might want to check the BASIC manual that came with your computer to see which functions are available on your system.

INT is a function that changes any number that you supply into a whole number or integer. For example INT(4.5) will return the value 4. For numbers greater than 0, INT just throws away any fractions and supplies you with the whole number.

Loops are sections of programs that may be repeated more than once — usually a specified number of times, or until certain conditions are met. For example, if you wanted to write a program that would count from 1 to 100, a loop could be used to keep adding 1 to a counter variable until the number 100 was reached. Loops are most commonly formed with FOR/NEXT statements or GOTO commands. You'll find many examples of these in the programs in this book.

Random Number Generator This function, which is called RND in BASIC, lets you generate numbers at "random" just as though you were throwing a set of dice and didn't know which number was going to come up next. In most home computers, the RND function returns a fraction between 0 and 1. To get numbers in a larger range, the program must multiply the fraction by a larger number. For example, RND * 10 will produce numbers between 0 and 10.

REM This command is used to tell the computer that whatever is on a particular line is just a comment or a remark and should not be executed. An example might look like this:
10 REM THIS PROGRAM COUNTS DOWN.

Variables are names used to represent values that will change during the course of a program. For example, a variable named D$ might represent any day of the week. It may help you to think of a variable as a storage box, waiting to receive whatever information you want to put in. Variables that deal with strings of characters are always followed by a dollar sign. Variables that end in a percent sign always hold integers (whole numbers like 1, 2, 3, 500). Variables with a pound sign or no special character at the end hold numbers that may contain fractions. The number of characters allowed in a variable name varies from computer to computer.

MASTER LISTS

The programs in the text are designed to run on the Apple II+ and IIe, but they will run on the IBM PC and PCjr, Radio Shack TRS-80 and Color Computer, Commodore-64 and VIC-20, and Atari with certain modifications. Below are Master Lists for each computer. These lines of programming customize the programs in the text for each computer. You will not need all of the lines in the Master List for each program. This Reference Manual will tell you which lines of the Master List are needed for each program.

If you can save programs on a disk or cassette, you can type in the Master Listing for your computer, give it a name, and save it. Then when you type in a program, simply load the Master Listing first, then type in the program for the text. Don't retype any lines that are numbered 800 or higher.

Master List for Commodore-64

```
800   XC$=MID$(A$,SB,SE):RETURN
820   A$=A$+B$:RETURN
900   PRINT CHR$(147);:RETURN
910   POKE XT,HT-1:POKE YT,VT-1:
      POKE FG,Ø:SYS PL:RETURN
920   FOR WS=1 TO WT:NEXT:RETURN
930   RD=INT(RX*RND(1)+1):RETURN
940   GET KY$:IF KY$="" THEN KY$=NU$
950   RETURN
960   XT=782:YT=781:FG=783:PL=6552Ø:
      SW=4Ø:SH=24:NU$=CHR$(Ø):RETURN
```

Master List for VIC-20

```
800  XC$=MID$(A$,SB,SE):RETURN
820  A$=A$+B$:RETURN
900  PRINT CHR$(147);:RETURN
910  POKE XT,HT-1:POKE YT,VT-1:
     POKE FG,Ø:SYS PL:RETURN
920  FOR WS=1 TO WT:NEXT:RETURN
930  RD=INT(RX*RND(1)+1):RETURN
940  GET KY$:IF KY$="" THEN KY$=NU$
950  RETURN
960  XT=782:YT=781:FG=783:PL=6552Ø:
     SW=22:SH=22:NU$=CHR$(Ø):RETURN
```

Master List for Radio Shack Color Computer (Requires Extended BASIC)

```
800  XC$=MID$(A$,SB,SE):RETURN
820  A$=A$+B$:RETURN
900  CLS:RETURN
910  HZ=INT(HT-1+(VT-1)*32+Ø.5):
     PRINT @HZ,"";:RETURN
920  FOR WS=1 TO WT:NEXT:RETURN
930  RD=INT(RND(RX)):RETURN
940  KY$=INKEY$:IF KY$="" THEN
     KY$=NU$
950  RETURN
960  NU$=CHR$(Ø):SW=32:SH=16:RETURN
```

Master List for Radio Shack TRS-80

```
800  XC$=MID$(A$,SB,SE):RETURN
820  A$=A$+B$:RETURN
900  CLS:RETURN
910  HZ=INT(HT-1+(VT-1)*64+Ø.5):
     PRINT @HZ,"";:RETURN
```

```
920  FOR WS=1 TO WT:NEXT:RETURN
930  RD=INT(RND(RX)):RETURN
940  KY$=INKEY$:IF KY$="" THEN
     KY$=NU$
950  RETURN
960  NU$=CHR$(Ø):SW=64:SH=16:RETURN
```

Master List for IBM PC and PCjr

```
800  XC$=MID$(A$,SB,SE):RETURN
820  A$=A$+B$:RETURN
900  CLS:RETURN
910  LOCATE VT,HT:RETURN
920  FOR WS=1 TO WT:NEXT:RETURN
930  RD=INT(RX*RND(1)+1):RETURN
940  KY$=INKEY$:IF KY$="" THEN
     KY$=NU$
950  RETURN
960  SW=4Ø:SH=24:NU$=CHR$(Ø):RETURN
```

Master List for Atari

```
800  XC$=A$(SB,SB+SE-1):RETURN
820  A$(LEN(A$)+1)=B$:RETURN
900  PRINT CHR$(125);:RETURN
910  POSITION HT+1,VT-1:RETURN
920  FOR WS=1 TO WT:NEXT WS:RETURN
930  RD=INT(RND(Ø)*RX+1):RETURN
940  K=PEEK(KZ):IF K=255 THEN
     KY$=NU$:RETURN
950  GET #1,KW:KY$=CHR$(KW):
     POKE 764,255:RETURN
960  NU$=CHR$(Ø):SW=37:SH=24:
     KZ=764:KW=Ø:OPEN #1,4,4,"K:"
     :RETURN
```

PROGRAM 1: THE DECODER

What the Program Does

ACT used a special encoder program to send you this message. You can use your DECODER program to decode the message. Be sure to use only uppercase letters when you enter your message. When you have entered all the lines of the secret message, type "STOP" to exit the program.

How the Program Works

DECODER works by subtracting a certain number from the ASCII value of each letter in your secret message (M$). After subtracting, the program turns the result back into a letter. The number that is subtracted depends on the position of the letter in the line of text. This means that 1 is subtracted from the first letter, 2 is subtracted from the second letter, and so on. This number that is subtracted is kept in the variable KT. If KT gets bigger than 26, it is reset to 1. The result of the subtraction is kept in the variable T. Since we want to keep all the letters between A and Z, we check to see if T is less than the ASCII value of the letter A. If it is, we just add 26 to get it back in line. If there are numbers or special characters in our code, the program leaves them alone. Nothing is subtracted from them and KT does not change.

Modifications for Other Micros

For all computers except the Apple II+ and IIe, use lines 800 and 900 from the Master List for your computer.

Also make these changes for the following computers:

Atari:
```
105 DIM A$(80),L$(1),M$(80),XC$(1)
```

TRS-80 and Color Computer:
```
105 CLEAR 2000
```

PROGRAM 2: THE ELECTRIC FENCE

What the Program Does

The electric fence is a "visual effect" combined in a program you must debug. In order to open the gate, you must enter a known name. Unfortunately, someone tampered with the program. The gate remains electrified even when a correct name is entered.

How the Program Works

Lines 110 through 130 just set up the fence so that it is the right length for your microcomputer. The DATA statements in lines 410 and 420 are trimmed to fit your screen.

At line 140, you are prompted to input a name. There are four names on the list, so the program checks your name (M$) against each

of the names in the DATA statement at line
430. If a name matches, a "flag" (T) is set
to 11. You may think that that is a rather
strange number to which to set a flag. It might
be worth remembering.

Lines 190 through 260 just display the
electrified fence. This is done by alternating
lines of "---" with lines of "/ / /". At line 270
we check to see if the gate should be opened.
If T = 1, then we open it. Hey, wait! In line
170 we set T = 11 if the name was valid. Why
are we setting it to T = 11 and checking for
T = 1? Someone must have tampered with the
flag setting in line 170. Change the line so that
T is set to 1 if a name matches. Try the program again.

Lines 290 through 380 display the gate
opening. You can slow up the electric fence
by changing the value of WU in line 970 to a
larger number. A smaller number will speed
up the effect.

Modifications for Other Micros

For all computers except the Apple II +
and IIe, use lines 800, 820, 900, 910, 920, and
960 from the Master List for your computer.

Also make these changes for the following computers:

Atari:
1Ø5 DIM A$(5Ø),B$(5Ø),BL$(5Ø),

```
        E$(5Ø),M$(15),N$(5Ø)
1Ø6   DIM NU$(1),X1$(15),XC$(5Ø)
```

TRS-80 and Color Computer:
```
1Ø5 CLEAR 2ØØØ
```

PROGRAM 3: ROUTE CHECK

What the Program Does

This program will check a possible presidential route for potential disaster. It will
display the map of the route, then check it.

How the Program Works

This program uses DATA statements to
define a map. The DATA statements are in
lines 410 through 430. Each DATA statement
defines a part of the route. At line 110 we read
in the three routes (R1$, R2$, R3$). The first
half of the route is always R1$. The last half
can be either R1$ or R2$. That decision is
made in line 170. The program now uses R2$
as the second half of the route. To use a dif-
ferent route, change line 170 to set A$ = R3$
for the second half of the route.

Since there are two parts to this program, drawing the map and checking the route,
we use the variable ZZ to indicate which part
of the program we are on. While ZZ is zero,
we are working on drawing the map. When ZZ

is one, we are checking the map. The difference is which symbol is used to draw, and whether we are checking for trouble along the way.

Modifications for Other Micros

For all computers except the Apple II+ and IIe, use lines 800, 900, 910, and 960 from the Master List for your computer.

Also make thse changes for the following computers:

Atari:
```
105  DIM A$(80),NS$(1),NU$(1),
     R1$(80),R2$(80),R3$(80),XC$(1)
970  WU=60:RETURN
```

IBM PC and PCjr, Commodore-64, VIC-20:
```
970  WU=100:RETURN
```

TRS-80:
```
105  CLEAR 2000
970  WU=60:RETURN
```

Radio Shack Color Computer:
```
105  CLEAR 2000
970  WU=100:RETURN
```

PROGRAM 4: TERMINAL LOGIN

What the Program Does

In order to break into BRUTE's terminal control program you must do two things. First you must discover the password that allows you to access the program, and second, you must give yourself enough time to enter the password. The program has a destruct sequence, so that, once accessed, you have only a limited time to enter the password. You must enter it PERFECTLY. The first spelling error will cost you your life! Read on to find out how to give yourself a little more time to enter the password.

How the Program Works

Program setup is done in line 110. At line 120, M is read from the DATA statement. M tells how many letters there are in the password. Next a letter is read from the data statement. At line 150 the keyboard is scanned for input, and the timer, T, is incremented. That timer, T, is the culprit. At line 160 it is compared to WU, your timer variable. If T has gotten larger than WU, the program goes to the destruct sequence. Can you see a way to give yourself 10 times as much time? What if you change line 160 to this? IF T>10*WU THEN 230

Okay, the timer is out of the way. What's

the password? We read a letter from a DATA statement in line 140. At line 170 we compare it to the input we got from the keyboard. If it's the same, we go to line 200 and increment a counter, K, and read another character from the DATA statement. Then we go back and compare with the next keyboard input. Can you find the six-letter password in the DATA statement? (It's at line 400.)

A few other things are happening in this program. Whenever there is no input from the keyboard, the timer keeps *ticking away*. At the first WRONG character you are sent to the "SO LONG, BUDDY!" statement, and the program ends.

Lines 270 through 390 are for special effects. When you get a correct login, BRUTE gives itself a rather presumptuous pat on the back. The loop at line 270 through line 330 causes the words BRUTE and LIVES to flash progressively faster in the middle of the screen. This display is followed by the words LOGIN COMPLETE in the middle of the screen just before the program ends.

Modifications for Other Micros

For all computers except the Apple II + and IIe, use lines 900, 910, 920, 940, 950, and 960 from the Master List for your computer.

Also make these changes for the following computers:

Atari:
```
1Ø5   DIM B$(15),KY$(1),NU$(1)
97Ø   WU=4Ø:RETURN
```

IBM PC and PCjr, Commodore-64, VIC-20:
```
97Ø   WU=5Ø: RETURN
```

TRS-80:
```
1Ø5   CLEAR 2ØØØ
97Ø   WU=3Ø:RETURN
```

Radio Shack Color Computer:
```
1Ø5   CLEAR 2ØØØ
97Ø   WU=3Ø:RETURN
```

PROGRAM 5: ELEVATOR

What the Program Does

ELEVATOR is a simple animation of an
elevator controlled by secret numbers. If you
type in one sequence, the elevator goes up.
Type in another sequence and it goes down.
Nothing happens if you type in the wrong
number sequence.

How the Program Works

Lines 100 to 110 are setup. Line 120 gets
the sequence for the elevator control. Lines 140
and 150 compare the sequence to the pro-

grammed numbers, 7235 and 5327. If neither number matches the input, the program goes back to line 120 for new input.

If 7235 matches the input, the program goes to line 170 where variables are set up for the elevator to move UP. If 5327 matches the input, the variables (A, B, and C) are set up to move the elevator DOWN. Either way, the program then clears the screen (line 180) and goes to the part of the program that "moves" the elevator.

Modifications for Other Micros

For all computers except the Apple II+ and IIe, use lines 900, 910, 920, and 960 from the Master List for your computer.

Also make these changes for the following computers:

Atari:
```
1Ø5   DIM B$(7),BL$(7),KD$(1Ø),
      NU$(1),SD$(7),T$(7),TL$(7)
97Ø   WU=25: RETURN
```

IBM PC and PCjr, Commodore-64, VIC-20:
```
WU=3Ø: RETURN
```

TRS-80:
```
1Ø5   CLEAR 2ØØØ
97Ø   WU=2Ø: RETURN
```

Radio Shack Color Computer:
1Ø5 CLEAR 2ØØØ
97Ø WU=3Ø:RETURN

PROGRAM 6: SHOOT-OUT

What the Program Does

SHOOT-OUT is a really fun arcade game. There are robots in the middle of the room that you must destroy. You have one half-intelligent robot to help you. This robot can move only around the perimeter of the room, and can fire into the room. You tell him when to fire by pressing the "F" key. Plan your moves carefully. You'll run out of bullets if you fire too carelessly.

How the Program Works

Lines 290 to 320 move your robot around the perimeter of the room. If you press the "F" key, it is detected at line 330, and the fire sequence takes place from line 350 to 410. An asterisk (*) is moved across the screen from the start fire position to the end fire position. After the bullet crosses the room, a call to the subroutine at line 510 checks to see how many robots have been killed with that bullet. It also checks to see if you have killed all the robots and determines if you have any bullets left.

If you want to make the game easier or harder to play, change the number of robots or bullets in line 120.

Modifications for Other Micros

For all computers except the Apple II+ and IIe, use lines 900, 910, 920, 930, 940, 950, and 960 from the Master List for your computer.

Also make these changes for the following computers:

Atari:
```
1Ø5  DIM DH(4),DV(4),EF(4),KY$(1),
     NU$(1),QH(4),QV(4),SF(4)
97Ø  RETURN
```

IBM PC and PCjr:
```
97Ø  RANDOMIZE (VAL(RIGHT$(
     TIME$,2))):RETURN
```

Commodore-64 and VIC-20:
```
97Ø  RD=INT(RND(-TI)):RETURN
1Ø5 CLEAR 2ØØØ
97Ø RETURN
```